Hailey tensed ~~immediately~~ ~~she~~ shouldn't have questioned her instincts after the armed robbery they'd just survived.

"Look, just because I'm not a cop anymore doesn't mean I've forgotten how to do my job," she said. She grabbed the bank's door handle and yanked. It didn't move. She pulled harder. "The door's locked."

Caleb tried the back door. It didn't open either. Were they locked in?

The air was thicker now. The hiss he'd been hearing had grown louder. A thin trail of smoke was seeping out from underneath one of the shelves. He pulled the shelf back. A green metal canister slipped free and spun like a top across the floor, propelled by the thin string of dark purple smoke hissing from the top. Block letters spelled out the chemical compound. KClO3. He turned back and ran toward Hailey.

"It's a smoke grenade!" Caleb yelled. "Potassium chlor—"

A bright orange flash lit up the air by his feet as it detonated...

USA TODAY bestselling author **Maggie K. Black** is an award-winning journalist and self-defense instructor. She's lived in the United States, Europe and the Middle East, and left a piece of her heart in each. She now makes her home in Canada, where she writes stories that make her heart race.

Books by Maggie K. Black

Love Inspired Suspense

Undercover Protection
Surviving the Wilderness
Her Forgotten Life
Cold Case Chase
Undercover Baby Rescue

Unsolved Case Files

Cold Case Tracker
Christmas Cold Case
Dangerous Arson Trail
Christmas Under Threat
Crime Spree Secrets

Mountain Country K-9 Unit

Crime Scene Secrets

Dakota K-9 Unit

Cold Case Peril

Visit the Author Profile page at LoveInspired.com for more titles.

CRIME SPREE SECRETS

MAGGIE K. BLACK

LOVE INSPIRED SUSPENSE
INSPIRATIONAL ROMANCE

INSPIRATIONAL ROMANCE

Recycling programs
for this product may
not exist in your area.

ISBN-13: 978-1-335-95771-9

Crime Spree Secrets

Copyright © 2026 by Mags Storey

Love Inspired
22 Adelaide St. West, 41st Floor
Toronto, Ontario M5H 4E3, Canada
www.LoveInspired.com

HarperCollins Publishers
Macken House, 39/40 Mayor Street Upper,
Dublin 1, D01 C9W8, Ireland
www.HarperCollins.com

Printed in Lithuania

Commit thy works unto the Lord,
and thy thoughts shall be established.
—*Proverbs* 16:3

To Stacey

ONE

Hailey Blue's fingers tightened on the steering wheel as she carefully maneuvered the armored truck down the beautiful Amethyst Harbour shoreline toward the small community bank to pick up the weekly deposits. The small town sat on the outskirts of the larger city of Thunder Bay, and the blue waters of Lake Superior shimmered to her right, dotted with the tree-lined shores of islands and islets, leading to the Michigan border beyond. To her left, local stores and businesses lined the street.

Hard to believe that a place this beautiful could be in the middle of a reckless spree of armed robberies. In the passenger seat, her colleague Jet Tailer's knee was bouncing so hard that she could hear his gun clacking in his holster. The man was nervous about their impending pickup. Then again, so was she. In fact, in all the years she'd worked as an armed security guard and a police officer before that, she'd never been this tense about what should've been a routine job.

Lord, how can I do this job, knowing that at any moment some rubber-masked criminal might suddenly try to murder me?

And leave her four-year-old son, Ferris, alone without a parent to raise him?

It had been two weeks since a pair of heavily armed thieves had started a spree of brazen daylight robberies in the remote northern city of Thunder Bay and the surrounding area, focusing on high-valued targets—all while wearing goat masks. They went by "Billy" and "Gruff," and their thefts were erratic. The first was at a pawnshop downtown, where the Goats had somehow managed to slip something in the security guard's soup, so he was too sick to see straight when they broke in. Two days later, they piped carbon monoxide into the ventilation system of a community bank in Fort William before robbing the place. But ever since then, they'd simplified matters and just burst in, holding guns and threatening to shoot anyone who didn't hit the floor fast enough or tried to fight back. Several innocent people had been seriously injured so far. It was only a matter of time before someone was killed.

Fear had descended over the entire area like a thick but invisible fog, prickling on her skin and sending shivers down her spine. People in Thunder Bay and nearby towns like this one were upping their security. Employees were calling in sick, including the colleague she was currently covering for. But Hailey had been raising Ferris on her own ever since he was born, after his father made it clear he wanted nothing to do with either of them. It was her responsibility to provide for her son. She couldn't just quit her job with the armed security firm, even if her friends were begging her to.

And yes, it was true that Hailey no longer wore a police badge. She'd turned it in and quit the force five years ago, reeling with the stress of the triple tsunami of her unexpected pregnancy, the man she loved leaving her and the murder of one of their closest friends. But those words she'd once pledged—to serve and protect her community, preserve peace and stop criminal offenses to the best of her ability—were still emblazoned on her heart.

"We've got a problem!" Jet's voice rose so quickly the man practically shouted. His hand flung across the front seat and probably would've instinctively grabbed the steering wheel if she hadn't raised an elbow to block him.

Quickly, she checked the mirrors and hit the brakes. The heavy, armored vehicle lurched to a stop. "What's wrong?"

"There's a potential hostile!" Jet said. "Strong-looking guy. Don't recognize him. Just pacing up and down the street, talking to himself."

He pointed and she followed his gaze, only to feel relief, confusion and a dozen other conflicting emotions crash over her heart at once. Jet had gestured to an impossibly handsome man who was apparently trying to carry on a conversation with someone through a small earpiece while also wrangling an unwieldy black-and-tan puppy in a K-9 vest.

It was Caleb Perry.

The son of the local police chief. Not to mention Ferris's father and the man who'd broken her heart then disappeared from her life.

She took a calming breath. "Nothing to worry about," she said, and started driving again. "That's just Police Chief Perry's son. He's an officer on the Ontario Cold Case Task Force. They solve old crimes that nobody else can." At least according to both gossip and the local news.

Judging by the gangly dog's K-9 vest, Caleb had made good on all the big career dreams and goals he'd moved 850 miles away from her for. He'd always been a remarkably good-looking guy, with broad shoulders, blond hair and dazzling blue eyes. But there was something different about him now. It was like he stood taller. He'd lost his baby-faced cuteness and the lines of his jaw were stronger. At thirty, it seemed he'd grown into himself.

Did that mean he was finally ready to step up and talk to her about being in Ferris's life?

A surge of conflicting emotions began to swell at the edges of her heart, like giant competing waves beating against the hulls of an already patched up wooden ship. She swallowed a breath and gritted her teeth. No, she wouldn't think about that now. Not while she had her gun in her holster, her bright blue uniform on and the responsibility to safely transport hundreds of thousands of dollars.

"His cousin Phoebe is getting married this weekend," Hailey added. "The rehearsal is tomorrow night. I guess he's here for the wedding."

Even though Phoebe had assured Hailey that he wasn't invited. Phoebe wasn't just Caleb's cousin, she was also Hailey's best friend. It had been her twin brother Matty's murder that had shaken up all their lives years ago. Her best friend was a widow and single mom who'd seen more than her fair share of tragedy before Daryl, the manager of the family cleaning company Phoebe now owned, had swept her off her feet and promised to make all of her dreams come true.

As if on cue, Caleb turned and walked away toward Pine Suds Cleaning, probably to go see Phoebe, Daryl or another one of their friends who worked there.

Jet cracked his knuckles. "So, that's the lowlife who took off to Toronto and left you to raise a kid on your own?"

Technically, yes. But the reality was so much more complicated than that, as realities usually were. When she'd called him to tell him that she was pregnant, he'd told her that Ferris wasn't his kid and accused her of cheating on him with Matty. Which wasn't only completely untrue but also downright cruel, considering Matty had just been killed. She'd screamed at Caleb and hung up on him. They hadn't spoken since.

Then a new thought hit her, momentarily knocking the bitterness aside and filling her heart with unexpected hope—was it possible that Caleb and his team were in town to solve Matty's murder?

"If he keeps hanging around, do you want me and Gordo to give him a talking-to?" Jet's hand slapped his holster. Gordo was the colleague she was covering for today. Like Jet, Gordo was in his early twenties and had played football in high school. She also suspected Gordo had a drug habit, considering how erratic his moods could be and how often he called in sick.

"No, thank you. It's fine." Hailey smiled awkwardly at the suggestion she might want or need to be rescued. Then again, she was a blond-haired woman with green-blue eyes. Not being taken seriously was par for the course. "Caleb is a really good guy."

Despite the fact that he somehow believed the worst about her. She wasn't a cheater, a liar or a sneak. Considering how close she and Caleb had been, she'd expected him to know that—immediately and without question. She'd been angry with him for a long time after their last conversation. But, she also knew how much pain he'd been in. Matty wasn't just his cousin, he was Caleb's best friend... and he'd died. Still, she'd been shocked, in pain and grieving too.

She steered the truck down the narrow alley that led to the back door of the bank and pulled the armored truck to a stop just in front of the door. Only then did she realize that she'd been gripping the steering wheel so hard that she could feel its grooves press against her skin. The alley was dark and narrow, with tall brick walls on either side that seemed to block out the warm spring sun.

The door was already open for them. A faint warning brushed her spine. The back door should've been closed.

"Hang on a second," she said. "The back door's open. Should we call into the bank and check everything's okay?"

"Nah," Jet said and shoved open his door. "They always do that. It's no biggie."

Maybe not, but it also wasn't protocol. Then again, this wasn't one of her regular stops and she was just here covering for Gordo. Before she could respond, Jet hopped out and strode around to the back of the truck. She closed her eyes and prayed.

Lord, free my heart from distractions, keep me safe from anyone who might want to harm me and help me focus on just getting this pickup done—

A loud and panicked shout cut through the moment of peace.

"Jet?" she shouted, leaping out and running around to the back of the van. "Jet, are you alright?"

A muffled bang shook the alley and bounced off the walls. Her heart raced. She yanked her weapon out, reaching the back of the van, and saw Jet lying dead on the ground.

For a second, Hailey's world froze as her baffled eyes took in the scene.

A man in a white goat mask stood over Jet's body, looking down at what he'd done. Smoke still rose from the barrel of the silencer of his gun. As for Jet, her colleague was beyond help. Tragically—and maybe also mercifully—the single gunshot had been instantly fatal.

Time sped up again as she raised her weapon high, holding it firm with both hands, and aimed it right at the masked gunman.

"Drop the gun!" she ordered. "Put your hands up and step away from the body!"

Jet's killer startled and the weapon almost slipped from his hand, as if he'd been stunned by seeing her there. Perhaps he hadn't known that Platinum's security officers always worked in pairs. Or maybe he wasn't expecting Jet's partner to be a woman. They stood eye to eye—he was barely two inches taller than her own five-foot-four-inch frame. He hesitated.

Lord, guide my words and my hands.

There had to be at least half a dozen innocent civilians in the bank right now, all of whom needed her help if they were going to make it out of here alive.

"Billy!" A deep and angry male voice boomed from somewhere through the open door. It had an uncanny and distorted echo. "What's going on out there? Let's get this show on the road!"

The Billy Goat turned toward the voice, which gave her the tiniest chance to escape and get help. She'd take it. Her eyes darted from the van on her right to the end of the alley far to her left and she made the split-second decision to run for the vehicle. Shouting and swearing erupted behind her. Hailey didn't let herself look back. She'd almost reached the van door when a man in a gray goat mask charged around the front of the van forward her. Guess this would be Gruff.

"Stop right there, Hailey Blue," Gruff ordered, "or I'll shoot you where you stand!"

She froze. He knew her name. Guess they'd done their homework after all. Did they also know she had a son? The chill that cut through her chest grew deeper. Gruff's voice was deep, distorted, as if by some kind of vocal box, and carried a hint of menace that made her absolutely certain he wouldn't hesitate to make good on his threat. The sound of footsteps behind her told her that Billy, the white-masked goat, had reached her too, even before she felt the cold edge of his gun pressed up against the base of her neck. She was trapped between them.

"Shoot her," Gruff ordered. "Now."

"No, wait!" Instinctively, her hands rose. Her gun dangled lose from her index finger. "I can get you the week's deposits and help you load them up. Just let the hostages go, and I'll get you the cash. Nobody else needs to get hurt."

The money would be covered by insurance. But the human lives inside the bank were invaluable. The Goats hesitated. Silently, she prayed for God's help and mercy.

Finally, Gruff shrugged.

"Fine," he said. "But no funny business, and don't even think about trying to call for help. Or we will kill you along with everyone else in there. And then we'll find and murder your son."

Caleb's K-9 trainee suddenly let out a warning bark that cut a chill through Caleb's core like a knife. The six-month-old Belgian Malinois was going squirrelly and Caleb had no idea why. The sunny spring day in Amethyst Harbour couldn't be more picturesque or peaceful. And yet Sheb was tugging at his leash and spinning around in circles, like he knew that something was terribly wrong and couldn't figure out how to communicate it.

Is something actually wrong, Lord? If so, what aren't I seeing?

"Sit!" Caleb commanded, holding his hand high. "Quiet!"

The puppy responded with a defiant and resounding howl.

"What's wrong?" Jackson Locke's voice came in Caleb's earpiece.

"Everything okay?" Gemma Craft—Jackson's sister—

chimed in at the exact same moment, so the siblings' voices overlapped.

Jackson was a K-9 officer and Gemma was a private detective. The siblings were not only members of the Ontario Cold Case Task Force, they were two of his closest friends.

"I don't know," Caleb admitted. It was like his K-9 trainee malfunctioned sometimes. Their boss, Inspector Ethan Finnick, who'd once led a RCMP K-9 unit before branching out to head of the Ontario Cold Case Task Force, had recently pulled some strings to get Caleb partnered with the unruly pup. Sheb—short for Shebandowan—was a smart dog. Sheb had a major K-9 test coming up on Monday and knew everything he needed to ace his K-9 training. But, it was like sometimes Sheb couldn't put it all together to tell Caleb what he needed to know. "One moment, we're enjoying the sunshine and the—*Oof.*"

Suddenly, the wind was knocked out of him as Sheb leaped up on his hind legs and shoved Caleb in the stomach with both paws, as if trying to force him back down the street.

"Sounds like he senses danger," Jackson said and the unmistakable chill of a warning cut through his tone. Jackson was an experienced K-9 cop, and Hudson, his German shepherd partner, was one of the most elite K-9s in the province. Sheb's breed looked like a smaller and leaner version of Hudson's.

"Agreed," Caleb said. "But I don't see anything or hear anything."

Caleb prayed for wisdom and looked down at the dog

"Show me," Caleb commanded. Sheb whined and sat down. Caleb sighed.

Caleb sat down on the edge of a planter and ran his hand over the dog's head. Sheb whined softly.

"He's stopped alerting," Caleb told his friends. He glanced at the front of Pine Suds, the cleaning company his aunt had started when Caleb and his friends were in high school. After her death a couple years ago, his cousin Phoebe had taken over…which brought him back to why he was in his hometown—the suspicious wedding invite he'd received in the mail with no return address.

Not that the mystery of who had invited Caleb to Phoebe's wedding was on the scale of the serial killers and criminals the Cold Case Task Force normally solved. Still, when he'd showed up in town, called his cousin and discovered that she had most certainly *not* invited him, he'd realized that somebody had tricked him into driving fifteen hours for nothing. Before he went home, he planned to stop at Pine Suds and speak to his cousin's fiancé, Daryl. He'd also hopped on the phone to get his friends' advice about what to do—it was the first time he'd told anyone about Hailey and their disastrous breakup. He knew the welcome home wouldn't be a warm one…all his old friends had remained close with her over the years, while he'd neglected to stay in touch even with his parents after skipping town.

Back then, the shock of Matty's death had had him in a grip, and he'd been getting ready to ship out to Toronto to join the RCMP anyway. He wasn't looking for anything serious…or maybe he'd been terrified that if he married her, he'd end up staying in Amethyst Harbour for the rest of his life, becoming a local cop and following in his father's footsteps. Probably didn't help that some of the guys had teased him since kindergarten about how "pampered" and "protected" he was, on account of who his dad was—even before his dad was promoted to chief of police when Caleb was in high school.

Back then, he'd lived his whole life in his dad's shadow, and it had felt like he'd never step up, become his own man and be respected for who he was, instead of who he was related to.

Sheb's ears perked again. The dog sat up sharply.

Then, a faint pop echoed from somewhere farther down the street. A shiver ran down Caleb's spine. Sheb leaped up and began to howl. Was that a handgun?

He signaled the dog to show him where the sound had originated from, but the dog's woofs rose, sharper and more urgent. Caleb prayed silently and his eyes scanned the street, searching for any sign of trouble. Then something caught his eye—the bank at the end of the block had lowered its blinds. He was sure they'd been open when he'd walked past it earlier.

"Everything okay?" Jackson asked. His voice had snapped from concerned friend to cop in an instant.

"No," Caleb said. "I think there's something going on at the bank. The blinds are down. And come to think of it, I spotted an armored truck pulling in a few minutes ago. Maybe we've got a robbery."

Or it might be nothing. A random gunshot in the distance wasn't the kind of thing people called the police about in a northern town, and there were a lot of innocent reasons a bank's blinds could be down.

The only evidence he really had that something was wrong was his K-9 trainee. And Sheb was less than reliable.

Still, he began to run down the street toward the bank. Sheb sprinted ahead of him, tugging on the leash.

"Location?" Gemma asked and he could hear her typing, even as he rattled off the bank's address.

"I'd advise you to approach cautiously," Jackson said.

"Agreed," Caleb said. Which was going to be pretty

hard to do with how rambunctious Sheb was. There was a coffee shop on his right, exactly where he'd remembered, but with a different look and name than the one that had been there last time he'd been in town. He entered the shop and clocked eight people sitting at various tables and two behind the counter. He recognized most of them. Caleb pulled his badge.

"I'm Corporal Caleb Perry of the Ontario Cold Case Task Force," he said, loudly. "There's been a possible disturbance at the bank and I need to leave my K-9 Sheb here for a moment to go check it out. He's a good dog, bit energetic but really friendly."

"No problem," a man with a long brown beard called from behind the counter. "Is it the Goats?"

Goats?

"I don't know," Caleb admitted.

He left Sheb in the care of the barista, pushed back through the door and ran toward the bank.

"Ever heard of something called the Goats?" he asked Jackson and Gemma.

"No," Gemma replied. Typing sounded down the line. "Yes! Got it. Local crime spree. Two men in goat masks have hit a handful of high-value targets in and around Thunder Bay in the past couple of weeks."

"Any targets in Amethyst Harbour?" he asked.

"No." The tension in Gemma's voice cut through the line. "But they've been expanding the radius of their attacks. No deaths yet but several gunshot wounds and serious injuries. I'm surprised your father never mentioned it."

"Dad and I don't talk that often," Caleb said, "and he has a policy against discussing work during 'family time.'" Instinctively, his fingers made air quotes, even though his friends couldn't see them. "Thunder Bay is a larger city and has its own police force. The last major crime to hit my dad's jurisdiction in Amethyst Harbour was Matty's murder."

"How was he murdered?" Gemma asked.

"Matty crashed his car into Lake Superior the night after a friend's wedding and drowned," Caleb said. He sighed, feeling a familiar sadness ache inside his heart like an old wound that had never fully healed. "Turned out he was drugged."

And Matty's final known words had been a voice memo he'd tried to send Caleb, confessing that Matty was the father of Hailey's child. Crime scene investigators had uncovered it from Matty's phone and played it for Caleb, even while Caleb was still processing the fact his cousin had been murdered.

He'd reached the bank now and muted the phone. The front blinds were drawn so tight he couldn't see in. Carefully, he tried the front door. It was locked. Somebody had even flipped the closed sign. Quietly, he moved to the side of the building, where he was finally able to glance through a tiny gap between the curtain and the frame to see what was happening inside.

The first thing Caleb saw were the dozen or so civilian hostages lying down on the floor of the bank, with their hands tied behind their backs, including an elderly security guard. A man in a gray goat mask stood over them.

He saw a woman in a blue uniform step out of the vault, holding on to large money bags in her hands. A blond braid fell down her back. A man in a white goat mask stepped into view, pressing a gun into the back of her head. She set the bags down. One fell over and money spilled out onto the floor.

"Turn around!" the man shouted. "Kneel!"

She knelt and her chin rose defiantly.

"Please!" she said. "Don't do this! I have a son!"

The Goat pressed the gun between her eyes. Caleb's heart caught in his throat as she tilted her head, and he could finally see the lines of her beautiful face.

It was Hailey.

TWO

The man in the goat mask intended to kill her, just like he'd killed Jet.

Hailey had absolutely no doubt about that. Despite how hard she might beg and plead for her son not to grow up without his mother.

Lord, help me find a way out. Please, save my life!

Yet, even as she knelt on the cold tile floor, with a gun pressed hard against her forehead and panic welling up inside her heart, she could also feel the investigative cop she'd once been trying to catalogue the clues she saw around them.

Billy was of average height, with huge combat boots, a black hoodie two sizes too big for him and leather gloves. Red mesh covered the mask's eyeholes and kept her from seeing his eyes. A hidden voice distorter made his voice unnaturally deep. He was twitchy too. Even as he aimed a gun between her eyes, she could see him bouncing on the soles of feet like he was in a hurry to get somewhere. Gruff, of larger build, was humming as he lumbered around the bank, rummaging through desks and drawers, occasionally waving his weapon back and forth in the direction of the hostages huddled on the far side of the room.

While both men seemed to have had a basic idea of the

layout of the building, neither of them had seemed all that focused or prepared, which tracked with the fact that so far they seemed to be figuring out their tactics on the fly, considering how their MO kept changing. Gruff and Billy had chuckled and joked with each other as they'd rounded the hostages up, as if the fear of their fellow human beings had meant nothing to them. They'd tossed bags of money around like cheap candy.

It was almost like they thought they were playing a video game.

In fact, if one of the hostages had been brave or foolish enough, they might've even been able to successfully disarm Gruff. Then again, they also could've been killed for their trouble.

A cold breeze whipped against her skin, like somewhere beyond the back storage area a door to the outside world had been opened and then shut again. Her eyes rose past the barrel of the gun now pressed against her forehead to where the door to the back offices lay open. Was it her imagination, or did she hear the faint creak of footsteps in the back rooms?

Either way, neither Goat seemed to have noticed. She inhaled a deep breath, chose to believe that help lay just beyond the doorway and that if rescuers weren't coming to her, she'd make her way to them. She may not be the strongest person in the world. But she'd also never been the kind to give up without a fight.

"Come on!" Billy yelled across the bank to Gruff. "Let's go!"

"Gimme a minute!" Gruff didn't look up. "I want to make sure I don't miss anything good."

"Hey." Hailey lowered her voice and looked up at Billy. "I have gold bars and jewelry in a lockbox in the truck."

This was true. It wasn't that much and only a fraction of who men had raked in from the vaults. But Billy seemed to be itching to leave the bank and might be greedy enough to be lured back outside for it.

Billy tilted his head to the side and the mask shifted. He glanced at Gruff, then back to Hailey. "Yeah?"

"Yeah." She nodded and he pulled the gun back a few inches from her skin. "It's the kind of stuff that's really easy to pawn."

He didn't answer, but she sensed he was considering it.

"You won't be able to get it open," she went on, "but how about I open it for you, and you let me go?"

She didn't ever expect that he would live up to his side of the bargain. But she didn't need him to. Her plan was to escape and find help, and failing that, she'd have a much better shot at disarming one masked gunman than two. They'd taken her gun and looted Jet's body as well, but still she'd find some way to fight back. Her life and Ferris's depended on it.

"Okay, come on," Billy barked. "Get up, pick up the bags and don't try anything funny."

She stood slowly, grabbed a bag of cash with each hand and began to walk toward the door, praying for God's help with every step. Billy watched Hailey like a hawk, keeping the gun pointed at her head as she stepped in front of him, then he moved behind her and pressed the gun against her back. She set her eyes on the open door that led into the private employee area, and hoped with all her heart that there really was someone lurking back there who wanted to help. Her limbs were shaking so hard, it took all her strength to stop herself from spilling the overstuffed bags, stay calm and keep moving forward.

She walked through the doorway and found herself in a

large and nondescript office space, with a couple of small glass-topped desks and a kitchenette with a coffee maker. In the middle of the room sat a table and chairs. Several rows of green metal shelves stood beyond that, filled with files and boxes. Behind them, she could see the bright orange glow of the exit sign.

"Hey!" Gruff's deep and distorted voice bellowed from behind them. "What are you doing?"

She felt the pressure of the gun leave her back and heard the sound of Billy's footsteps stop, but she didn't risk looking back at him.

"Hailey says that there's gold and stuff in the truck," Billy called, and there was something stomach-churning about hearing his mechanical voice say her name. He sounded slightly annoyed, maybe at having to share the new loot.

She inched forward, one teeny tiny step at a time, trying to stretch out the distance in between her and the gun. She reached a table. It was made of thin plywood and would be pretty much useless in shielding her from a bullet. The kitchenette counter was sturdier, but it was all the way on the other side of the room. A movement ahead caught her eye. Someone was there, moving quickly between the shelves and then dropping out of sight.

"She's lying," Gruff shouted.

"No," Billy called back. "She's not!"

Their voices rose and overlapped.

"She's trying to trick you!" Gruff shouted. "Just shoot her in the head and let's go!"

And Hailey's gut said that was her signal to run. She flung the bags of stolen cash as far as she could in opposite directions, hoping he'd get flustered. Hailey sprinted toward the relative shelter of the shelves in an attempt to put some kind of obstacle between herself and the men's trigger fingers.

Curses and threats rose behind her and she was still half a room away from protection. Then came the first gunshot blast. Her feet stumbled as she expected to feel a bullet rip through her body. Instead, splinters showered her back as it tore through the plywood table. When the next shot came she might not be as fortunate.

Help me, Lord! Please, save my life!

For a moment, it was like the world froze around her. She could see her small son's face floating before her mind's eye, with his mop of blond hair and startlingly bright blue eyes, and she prayed desperately that she'd make it home to him safe. Then the memory of seeing Caleb on the street flashed before her eyes too. She asked God to forgive her for never pressing him to build a relationship with their son and hoped it wasn't too late.

Something moved behind the shelving again, and her heart startled to see Ferris's father—with the same unmistakable blue eyes, dimpled chin and blond, unruly hair. Caleb was crouching low behind the shelves.

She blinked. Was he really there? She didn't see the dog he'd had earlier and hoped it was okay.

Caleb's eyes met hers with a gaze that was strong and unwavering. His mouth moved in a silent warning. *Get down!*

Then, as she watched, Caleb threw himself against the closest metal shelf, sending it toppling over into the one beside it. Hailey threw herself sideways and rolled as the whole row of shelves came crashing down in an avalanche, smashing into each other and tumbling toward the gunmen like dominoes.

When Caleb had decided to send the shelves cascading over, he hadn't expected just how loud it would be. Or how destructive. Hailey darted to his right and vanished from his sight, as boxes and files poured across the floor. The Billy Goat roared as shelves barreled into him, knocking him off his feet. A hole punch flew into one of the glass-top desks, shattering it.

Gruff clutched a bag of money to his chest and ran through a doorway to the front of the bank. The door slammed behind him. Caleb scanned the wreckage for any sign of Hailey. He couldn't see her anywhere. Was she trapped? Was she hurt?

Prayers for her protection filled his heart, even as he saw Billy scramble back up to his feet and open fire, filling the air with the sound of gunshots and the clang of ricocheting bullets. Was Billy shooting at Hailey? For all Caleb knew, the guy was shooting at random. The volume of the Goat's rage momentarily overwhelmed the voice distorter reducing the sound to a loud, angry and animalistic cry.

Caleb ducked low behind the fallen shelves and began to make his way along the edge of the room, crawling on his stomach as he searched for Hailey. For years, he'd avoided letting the thought of her even cross his mind. But now, questions about her safety beat like a drum through his brain. Was Hailey okay? Injured? Dead? Trapped under the maze of heavy boxes and broken metal?

God, if You're listening, please help me find her and get her home safe to her kid.

As betrayed and angry as he'd felt when he'd heard Matty's own voice telling him that Hailey was pregnant with his child, Caleb still cared about her and her son.

Caleb reached a dead end and crouched there, blocked from going any farther by the very shelves he'd sent falling. Slowly, the Billy Goat stalked through the room, sweeping the barrel of his gun from left to right. Caleb held his breath as the man's footsteps creaked closer, hoping he wouldn't spot Caleb crouched under the limited protection of the fallen shelves.

Billy stopped and spun his weapon toward Caleb. The barrel was pointed directly at the center of Caleb's face. Billy was still several feet away with an obstacle course of debris between them. But still there was no way Billy would miss at that range.

"Gotcha!" Billy chuckled. "Any last words?"

Then it was as if everything happened at once. Billy's fingers moved on the trigger. Caleb leaped to his feet, knowing he'd rather die standing than down on the floor at a killer's mercy. But then he heard a fierce and magnificent cry fill the air as Hailey jumped out from underneath the kitchenette counter, launched herself at Billy from behind and smashed a lamp hard against his head.

Wow. Caleb startled. That was gutsy, unexpected, and also kind of impressive.

And she wasn't a cop anymore? How? When? Why?

Billy shouted in pain and swung toward Hailey, knocking her backward with a swift backhanded blow to the jaw. She cried out and fell to the ground. Billy's fist clenched around the gun in his hand as he whirled toward her, like he couldn't decide whether to strike her again or shoot. But before Billy could decide, Caleb tackled the robber around the waist. They hit the ground together. Caleb's head smashed against the remains of what had once been a chair, and stars filled his eyes. Billy scrambled back up to his feet. Caleb did too and readied himself to fight. But instead, the masked man turned on his heels, sprinted across the floor and threw himself through the back door that led out to the alley. There was the faint metallic sound of something hitting the floor. Had Billy dropped something?

"I know they're getting away!" Caleb waved both hands

in apparent frustration. "But I'm also unarmed. I don't even have my handcuffs on me, but I've called dispatch. Police will be here any minute and my team was coordinating with them when I went in."

Something hissed softly behind him, like a kettle that was getting ready to boil or a damaged fire extinguisher leaking gas. He glanced back and felt something itch in his throat, but he couldn't see anything suspicious. Caleb coughed.

"Okay, that's probably smart," she said. "They're really trigger-happy."

Hang on, was she agreeing with him?

"They killed my colleague Jet," Hailey added.

"I know. I'm sorry." He'd seen the young man's body on the way in.

"Thanks," she said. "We've got to go check on the hostages."

He turned back to see Hailey moving toward the door to the front part of the bank, which Gruff had left through.

"Agreed," he said. "Just be careful not to disrupt anything, and remember it's a crime scene."

It was the kind of thing he and his colleagues on the task force said to each other all the time. But Hailey tensed and prickled immediately. "Look, just because I'm not a cop anymore doesn't mean I've forgotten how to do the job."

She grabbed the door handle and yanked. It didn't move.

Heat rose to the back of his neck. "Hey, I didn't mean anything by it."

Somehow, as the words flew out of his mouth they sounded more defensive than he'd intended them to.

She pulled harder. "The door's locked."

"Are you sure?" he asked.

"Of course I'm sure."

Caleb bit his tongue and tried the back door. That one didn't open either.

Hang on, were they locked in?

The air was thicker now. The hiss he'd been hearing had grown louder. A thin trail of smoke was seeping out from underneath one of the shelves. He pulled the shelf back. A green metal canister slipped free and spun like a top across the floor, propelled by the thin string of dark purple smoke emitting from the top. Block letters spelled out the chemical compound. KClO3. He turned back and ran toward Hailey.

"It's a smoke grenade!" Caleb yelled. "Potassium chlor—"

A bright orange flash lit up the air by his feet as the grenade detonated.

THREE

For one fleeting moment, Caleb could see Hailey's face as she spun back toward him. Her aquamarine eyes were wide. Her limbs were tensed to fight. He'd always known she was pretty. A decent cop too. But even his most flattering memories of her didn't hold a candle to the strong, beautiful, vulnerable and fierce woman standing in front of him now.

Had she changed? Had he? Or had his bitterness over what happened just clouded his mind?

Then the grenade erupted into a tidal wave of smoke, sweeping through the room, Hailey was gone and all he could see was a thick purple haze. He heard her cough. Smoke stung his eyes and he blinked rapidly.

"You okay?" Hailey called.

"I'm okay." He tried to shine his cell phone's flashlight into the smoke. It didn't help. "You still good?"

"Yeah!" Hailey shouted. "You sure it's a potassium chlorate grenade?"

"Yes," he called back. No doubt mixed with some kind of sugar for ignition and a heavy dose of indigo dye. "It was listed on the canister."

He heard Hailey pray and thank God.

"How can you be thanking God right now?" he asked.

"Because if it was tear gas, we'd be in a lot worse shape."

He almost chuckled with surprise at her answer.

"Yup, that's true." Instinctively, he turned and ran for the back door with his hands out in front of him. The sound of Hailey thanking God and asking for help continued to slip through the dark purple swirls filling his eyes, and he found his heart touched by how easily this new version of Hailey prayed. His palms smacked against the door. It still didn't move. His eyes were watering now and his throat stung like he'd swallowed a live coal. He reared back and threw his shoulder into the door again. It budged, but only slightly.

"It's locked too?" Hailey called.

"Sure seems like it." Caleb tried again. Something metallic rattled. Outside the door, sirens grew louder. Police would be arriving soon, but even though the grenade wasn't lethal he didn't exactly want to hang out in a smoke-filled room and wait. "I think somebody used a bicycle lock on it from the other side."

"Crude and simple," Hailey said, "but effective. The Goats keep evolving their tactics with each crime. It's like they're leveling up."

"Does the other door budge at all?"

"No." Hailey's disembodied voice called back from across the room. "And I'd rather send the smoke out of the building than farther in."

"Agreed."

As bad as the irritation burned in his eyes and throat right now, that was nothing compared to what being hit with this much smoke would do to a hostage who was elderly, or had asthma or respiratory problems. He focused on keeping his breathing shallow. The sound of shuffling footsteps seeped through the haze.

"Hang on," Hailey said, "I'm coming to you. Maybe we can try some teamwork."

"Sounds good." It wasn't like the arguing would do them any good. He started making his way through the darkness toward the sound of her voice. "I'm going to try to meet you halfway. Be careful, okay? The floor is a wreck, so I'll try to clear a path on my side and guide you back."

"Just keep talking," she said, "and I'll find you like a dolphin using echolocation."

To his astonishment, he laughed—this time unable to stop the chuckle before it had left his throat. Then, he heard Hailey laughing back in response, which surprised him even more.

He continued to move through the cloud of smoke toward her, kicking debris under the way and calling out "Here" every few moments to guide her. Her voice grew louder too, until it sounded like they were only a foot or two apart. He stretched out his hands toward the sound of her voice, hoping to feel her there.

Suddenly, he heard her yelp sharply in pain and felt her body fall into his chest. He wrapped his arms around her quickly and held her to him. Her hair brushed up against his cheek. The smell of her filled his senses. She wrapped her hands around his neck, and he could feel her pulse was racing. His was beating just as fast.

"You okay?" he asked.

"Yeah," she said. The soft outline of her face hovered inches in front of his. "My foot just got caught on something. Give me a second and I'll wriggle it out."

But the moment she tried to pull away, she inhaled sharply and clutched at him again.

"My ankle is wedged in sideways," she said. He could tell she was trying to keep her tone light, but still, she couldn't hide the pain in her voice. "I can't put any weight on it or I'm worried it'll snap."

Sirens sounded from somewhere beyond the walls, along with shouting. Emergency lights trickled under the doors, flashing like lightning behind clouds of smoke. The cavalry had arrived.

"How can I help?" he asked her.

She hesitated for a moment before answering, as if desperately trying to find a better answer than the one she was about to give. Then she growled very softly under her breath in frustration. "I think you'd better hold on to me and keep me upright until rescue gets here. Sorry."

"No problem."

"Hopefully, it'll only take them a second." She sighed. "Ironically, I wasn't even supposed to be working here today. My colleague Gordo called in sick."

"Is that suspicious?" Caleb asked, instinctively.

"I don't think so. Maybe. He's unreliable and kind of erratic. I think he has a drug problem." She leaned against his chest and he tightened his grip around her. "How long have you been in town?"

Her voice sounded pinched, and he wondered if she was using small talk to distract herself from the pain.

"About an hour," Caleb said. "I got an invite to the wedding, then when I arrived and called Phoebe to tell her I was in town, she was surprised as she hadn't sent the invite."

"Now, that is suspicious," Hailey's voice rose. "I can't imagine Daryl would invite you without telling her."

"Me neither," Caleb said. Sure, Daryl had been one of the guys who'd teased him, but that didn't mean there was any bad blood between them. "I'm guessing it was my mom."

He relaxed slightly and she leaned deeper into his arms.

"You going to talk to your mom about it?" Hailey asked, and her tone softened.

His mom had begged him not to move to Toronto to pursue policing because of how "dangerous" the big city was, only to then guilt-trip him when Hailey had become pregnant about his "responsibility" to marry her, even after he tried to tell her he had reason to think the kid wasn't his. She was a social worker—and a good one—and he guessed all the bad situations she'd seen had made her overprotective. Add to that the fact his father had refused to let him know any of the nitty-gritty details about the investigation into Matty's murder, beyond the fact that wedding guests were being interviewed and everything was being done by the book.

He'd felt like his mom wouldn't listen and his dad wouldn't talk. At least not in the way he needed them to. And while Caleb hadn't exactly cut off contact with his parents after that, he'd definitely been distant.

"Probably not," Caleb admitted. "You know what she's like. Mom means well. But it's like she pushes me down the path she wants me to be on. Instead, I'll just take Sheb back to the motel, check out and drive back to Toronto."

He expected Hailey to point out that meant he'd end up driving a thirty-hour round trip, and that he should at least sleep the night. Or tell him off for avoiding conflict by not raising the wedding invitation thing with his mom. He even thought she'd maybe have encouraged him to talk to his parents or friends while he was in town.

Instead, all Hailey said was, "Your K-9's name is Sheb?"

He blinked.

"Yeah," he said. "Short for Shebandowan. All of our dogs on the task force are named after bodies of water."

There was a moment of silence and he wondered if she'd change the subject.

"That's really cool," she said.

Despite how awkward the moment was for both of them, she sounded genuine, and it reminded him of the easygoing, friendship-based romance they'd once had, before Matty had died and Caleb discovered Hailey had cheated on him and gotten pregnant.

"The other dogs on my team are all named after lakes," he went on, maybe to distract himself, "They're Simcoe, Nipissing and Michigan. Sheb's still in training and has a major K-9 test coming up on Monday. So, I have to be back in Toronto for that."

"Hmm," Hailey responded, leaving him with no clue how she felt about that.

Sad he wasn't sticking around longer? Happy he'd be leaving so soon?

Either way, he changed the subject to something safer.

"When did you stop being a cop and go into private security?"

"A few months after Matty died."

He wanted to ask her why, but was afraid he didn't want to hear the answer.

She shifted her position and he felt the top of her head brush against his cheek. "Are you and your team going to investigate Matty's murder?"

"I don't know," he admitted, feeling his guard actually fall for the first time since crossing the border into town. "Obviously, I want to. I'd love for my team to take a look at the case files and see if we can assist the local police in any way." It wasn't the reason he'd come home, but being back in town had him yearning for answers to questions he hadn't thought about in a long time. He'd buried the pain of Matty's untimely death years ago, along with any hope for justice. "My colleagues are absolutely incredible and some of the best people I've ever known. We're more than a team—we're friends, or even family. But, we only investigate cold cases, which for our unit means a case has to be about ten years old."

He could now hear somebody calling for bolt cutters outside the door. He glanced in the direction of the voices and heard the sound of the bicycle chain lock rattling. Any moment now and they'd be free.

"Look, I'm sorry about Matty," Caleb said, forcing the words he should've said years ago through his lips. "Despite everything that happened between us, I know you care about him a lot."

"Yeah." Hailey's voice sharpened. "Like you did—like a brother."

He recoiled. She was still lying to him? After all this time?

But her grip tightened around him.

"Caleb, listen to me," Hailey said. "Matty was protective and caring. I miss him every day, and I wish I'd paid more attention to everything that happened the night he died. I want his murder to be solved. But I loved him like a friend. Nothing more."

"Look, you don't have to lie to me anymore," Caleb's voice rose. "I've forgiven you!"

Or at least he was trying to.

"I didn't do anything I need to be forgiven for!"

The door flew open, smoke rushed out into the alley and police in protective gear stormed in. A tall and imposing man in his early sixties, with white hair, a thick mustache and a large gold badge hanging over his navy blazer, stepped in through the haze.

"Why, hello, son," Police Chief Sylvester Perry said, with a curious smile. "It's been a while."

It only took a few seconds for the officers to get her ankle free from the broken shelf it was trapped under. Then Caleb turned to talk to his dad, and Hailey found herself whisked off to an ambulance outside, where she spent another thirty-five minutes being checked out by the paramedics, before being given a clean bill of health except for a few scrapes and a mild sore throat. From there, it took her another forty-five minutes to give her detailed statement to a pair of investigators about Jet's murder and the Goats' robbery, and then get up to speed about what the police were able to fill her in on.

Law enforcement had removed Jet's body from the alley before breaking the door down and cordoning off the area. The hostages had all been taken to the hospital with non-life-threatening injuries. The two masked men had not been found, despite the fact they'd managed to spill a decent amount of money from their bags while making their escape, further cementing her theory that whoever they were, they weren't exactly pros. An officer then drove her back to Platinum Security for a professional yet emotional office-wide briefing by police about Jet's murder with her boss and colleagues—all except for Gordo, who was apparently not answering his phone. Her boss told her she could take tomorrow off work, but he needed her back the day after.

By the time she changed back into her jeans and T-shirt in the employee changing room, said goodbye to her colleagues and hopped into her car to go pick up Ferris, she'd been able to successfully push aside all of her inconvenient thoughts about Caleb for a good couple of hours.

But now, as she drove through the beautiful tree-lined

streets to her best friend Phoebe's house, there was nothing to stop the tsunami of conflicting emotions that rushed back into her heart with a vengeance. Especially since she was pretty sure Phoebe would want to talk to her about him. Phoebe had the softest and kindest heart of anyone Hailey had ever known, but she'd also pushed Hailey pretty hard to make peace with Caleb and get him involved in Ferris's life.

Maybe Hailey was just too proud to beg. But then again, how could Caleb possibly believe that she'd had a romantic relationship with Phoebe's brother Matty? Where had that idea even gotten into his head? Also, how was it possible that he was even more handsome now than when she'd last laid eyes on him? And why had her heartbeat started racing when he'd caught her in his arms? Had Caleb noticed that? Plus, Caleb told her himself that he was leaving town right away. It wasn't like he had any desire to sit down and talk things out with her...

Let alone ask to finally be a part of their son's life.

I didn't do anything I need to be forgiven for!

The words she'd shouted at him earlier niggled at the back of her conscience.

I never lied to him, Lord, and I definitely never cheated. But no matter how many times I felt You prompting me to pick up the phone or write an email to try to mend the chasm between me and Caleb, I always found a reason to put it off.

It wasn't like she'd never tried to tell Caleb about the fact they were going to have a child together. But during that phone call, she'd been struggling through a rough pregnancy and reeling from Matty's murder.

She'd discovered that she was pregnant the morning of her friends Renee and Lenny's wedding, and had tried to tell Caleb about it at the reception. Instead, before she'd managed to get the words out, he'd broken her heart and ended their relationship—apparently because he was moving to Toronto and didn't want anything long-distance. She'd been even more devastated, days later, when she'd tried again to tell him over the phone and he'd accused her of cheating on him. She'd cried for days, before finally picking herself up, turning her life and heart over to God, relying on her faith and her community, and moving on.

Besides, hadn't it been his responsibility to take the first step, call her and apologize?

Whenever she'd felt the still, small voice of God prompting her heart, she'd found a reason to put it off. She would wait until the pregnancy was viable, when the baby was born or when Ferris was sleeping through the night. She'd wait until after she'd left the police force and found a job with more regular hours that worked better with being a single mom. Above all, she told herself she'd wait until Caleb reached out to her first. And maybe she'd just kicked her fears farther and farther down the road, in the hopes she'd never have to face them.

Then today, she'd come face to face with the knowledge that her life could suddenly end in an instant—and then Ferris would be without a mother, and she could only hope that somebody else stepped up to bridge the chasm that had kept Caleb from meeting his son.

Guide me, Lord. Help me be brave.

She'd reach out to Caleb and talk to him. She'd face her fears and do what she knew God was calling her to do.

Tomorrow.

There couldn't be any harm in waiting one more night to have the conversation they needed to have. Right? After all, he was probably back on the road driving to Toronto by now, she was exhausted and they could talk over the phone.

When she pulled into the driveway of Phoebe's small two-bedroom house, she was relieved to see that their friend Renee Larkin's brand-new lilac SUV was parked in the driveway beside Phoebe's more modest old sedan. Where Phoebe was a tiny bundle of warmth and gentle curves, Renee was a tall and lithe rubber band of determination and energy. Whatever smoothie health fad or at-home money-making opportunity Renee had discovered this week, it would provide a perfect diversion from letting the conversation get too deep and emotional.

Hailey had never been as close to Renee as she was to Phoebe, but she'd known both women since kindergarten. Hailey had actually been at Renee and Lenny's wedding reception when Caleb had broken her heart. She'd just discovered she was pregnant that morning. Then she'd caught the wedding bouquet. Lenny, Daryl and even Matty had started teasing Caleb about how he had to turn down his acceptance with the mighty RCMP K-9 unit in Toronto and "settle" for a life of being a local cop with his dad.

This had led to a fight between her and Caleb. He'd ended their relationship. Matty had found her crying outside and taken her to a local diner where they'd sat for hours and she'd poured out her heart. Something had been off with Matty that night. He'd been even more emotional and impulsive than usual. It was only later she'd discovered he'd had sleeping pills in his system, but as nobody knew when he'd ingested them, it was hard to know how much that had influenced what he'd said to her that night.

Matty had told her he loved her, asked her to marry him and suggested they tell everyone the baby was his. It had been a grand, sudden and foolish gesture.

A sudden memory filled her mind.

I mean it! Matty had said. He'd reached across the table

and grabbed her hand. His dark eyes had looked sincerely into hers. *Caleb gets his big city job. You'll get a husband who'll love both you and your baby to his dying day! Everybody wins!*

She'd laughed him off, despite the tears that had filled her eyes, and hugged him. There was no way she'd have ever gone through with something like that, so she'd assumed he wouldn't have either. She wasn't a liar. She was sure Matty wasn't either. He definitely wouldn't have lied to people like that about her, even if his heart had been in the right place. Either way, it didn't matter, because he'd never gotten the opportunity to run around town proclaiming to their friends and family of his foolish desire to marry her.

After all, she'd been the last known person to see Matty alive.

She'd been questioned by police after Matty's death, of course, and although she'd admitted the contents of their last conversation, the investigators had promised to keep the details confidential. Chief Perry was an excellent cop; he ran a tight unit and wouldn't have ever allowed her personal life to be fodder for the gossip mill.

Help me, Lord. All I want is to put my past behind me, but it feels like it's looping right back around again.

She shoved the memory away, got out of the car, walked up to the front door and opened it. None of them ever locked their doors.

"Hello?" she called, brightly

She expected Ferris to charge down the hallway and into her arms. But instead, today she was greeted with an empty hallway and the sounds of happy children and lighthearted conversation filtering in from the small house beyond. She took off her shoes and found a spot for them in the jumble that crowded the front door. Phoebe lived in the same small and modest two-bedroom home that she and Matty had grown up in with their mom, Steff. Daryl had bought them a much larger and nicer one, which they'd move into after their wedding.

Daryl claimed to be the richest man in Amethyst Harbour—which was probably an exaggeration. But it was true he'd turned the family's flailing cleaning company around after Steff passed, made a tidy profit through investing in Renee's constant string of ventures and apparently managed to make enough money through online trades. He'd not only been able to splash out for the wedding of Phoebe's dreams but also a secret honeymoon surprise. Phoebe had gotten a passport for it. Not to mention a large and stunning engagement ring. Hailey had known Daryl, Renee and Renee's husband, Lenny, since elementary school too.

Hailey walked down the hall, following the sound of voices ahead. Pictures of Phoebe with her own fraternal twins, River and Lake, dotted the walls. Then she stopped at framed photo of another boy and girl with their mother—Matty, Phoebe and Steff. All three were holding matching pairs of giant scissors and cutting the ribbon of the cleaning company Pine Suds. She guessed Matty and Phoebe were about thirteen in the picture, with identical mops of curly brown hair, dark eyes and wide cheeky grins. Sadness pierced her heart. Steff had died of a heart attack when Matty and Phoebe were barely twenty. Then five years later, Matty had been murdered and Phoebe had been left alone in the world.

Lord, please bless my friend and fill her with happiness and joy. Don't let my own drama with Caleb get in the way of Phoebe's big day.

Not to mention the Goats and their crime spree.

"Hailey, hi! How long have you been standing there?"

Renee's voice called, cheerfully. Hailey turned to see Renee stepping through the kitchen doorway dressed in something long, flowy and floral, and carrying her baby, Luna, in a matching sundress.

"Only a minute." Hailey shook the sadness away, smiled and started toward her.

"How are you feeling?" Renee asked. Worry filled her eyes. "Lenny and Daryl both called and filled us in on what happened down at the bank. They were working at Pine Suds when it all went down, and apparently it was chaos. The street's still shut down."

Both Phoebe's fiancé and Renee's husband had been working at Steff's industrial cleaning company since high school. Phoebe and Matty had worked there too, and Phoebe was still in the office part-time. Back then, they'd all driven around in a big blue van with bubbles on the side and picked up people's carpets. They'd also maneuvered giant cleaners around office complexes at night. Now, Lenny was chief financial officer, Daryl was manager and head of client operations and Renee was one of the receptionists. Even Hailey had worked a few shifts on the overnight cleaning crews in between resigning from the police and landing her new role with Platinum Security.

She glanced past Renee down the hallway into the living room. "Where are the kids?"

"We put together a bowl of goodies for them and set them up in a blanket fort in the twins' room," Renee said. "We thought you might want some privacy without any little ones listening in."

"Thank you," Hailey said. "I really appreciate it."

Hailey leaned in to give her friend a half hug, and the six-month-old baby squealed and waved her pudgy arms toward her.

"Down for Luna snuggles?" Renee asked.

"Absolutely." Hailey reached out her hands, took the baby and nestled Luna into her arms. Luna cooed and cuddled against her.

"Now, come on," Renee said. "Before we start talking about anything serious, you got to see what a delivery man dropped off at Phoebe's front door an hour ago."

Renee turned and headed back into a well-worn but bright and cheerful kitchen.

"Phoebe!" Renee called and chuckled lightly. "Hailey is here to save us!"

Hailey followed, carrying the baby. "What do you all need saving from?"

"The ridiculously large basket of expensive chocolate and treats the reception venue sent," Phoebe said, with a laugh. She ran her hands down her blue jeans then reached for Hailey and gave her a long and warm hug, enveloping Luna as well. Phoebe was four foot eleven and her fiancé, Daryl, was barely three inches taller. But she hugged like a woman twice her size.

"I'm worried I won't be able to fit in my wedding dress on Saturday if I don't stop snacking." Then Phoebe stepped back and waved her hand toward the counter. "See for yourself."

The bright green wicker container was as big as a laundry basket, and was adorned with a mass of colorful ribbons and cellophane. It was teeming almost to the brim with bags of candies and chocolates in every shape and size, along with pretzels, cookies, chips and drinks. Hailey whistled. Well, now that was an unexpected distraction. "I can honestly say I've never seen a basket that big."

"You should've seen how full it was when it arrived," Phoebe said. "The kids, Renee and I have been nibbling ever since it was delivered and barely made a dent." She started pulling bags of gummy bears, candy peaches and watermelon candies out of the basket and stacking them on the counter. "Please, take all the sour ones. You're the only one I know who likes them. There are two cans of that sparkling grapefruit tea you like too. Honestly, take whatever you want. There's more than enough for three families."

"I'll say." Renee poured a handful of jelly beans into her hand. "They never sent me and Lenny anything like this basket for our reception." She popped them into her mouth.

Hailey reached for a grapefruit drink, cracked it open and took a sip. It fizzed lightly. She set it down again, and then turned Luna around in her arms, so that the baby could look at her mother and Phoebe.

"So, the guys called and told you what happened," Hailey said. "What did they tell you?"

Both of her friend's smiles faded.

"Rumor is that somebody from your company was killed," Phoebe said.

"Yeah," Hailey said. "His name was Jet. He was a really good guy. I was there when it happened."

"You saw it!" Renee gasped. "Do the robbers really wear masks? What are they like? They sound terrifying."

Phoebe's eyes widened. "Oh, honey! We thought you weren't working the bank job today! We thought you were supposed to be at that estate sale near Lakehead."

"I was," Hailey answered Phoebe's question first. Then she took another sip of the drink, as Renee took Luna and set her down in a play seat on the floor. Hailey popped a handful of sour candies into her mouth and leaned back against the counter. "My colleague Gordo called in sick so I went with Jet as a last-minute replacement."

She quickly filled them in on the bullet points of what

had happened, starting with arriving at the bank, to Jet being shot, to being taken hostage by the Goats, and finally to Caleb showing up, glossing over the facts he'd accused her of lying again and that she'd got her ankle stuck—and he'd had to hold her until help arrived.

"Lenny says Caleb was pacing the street outside Pine Suds," Renee said, "with a police dog, no less." She bit into a large peach gummy and chewed it slowly. "Honestly, I don't even know why you keep that dangerous security job. You should give up the whole security thing and come work with us at Pine Suds."

"Are you going to try and talk to Caleb about Ferris while he's in town?" Phoebe asked, and Hailey couldn't help but notice her friend wasn't meeting her eye.

It was such a simple question. But so many layers and complexities lay beneath the surface.

"I think he's already left town," Hailey said. "It sounds like his mom went around your back and sent him an invitation to your wedding."

"I guess so," the bride said, and her cheeks reddened. "He's my cousin and it would have been nice to have him at my wedding. But Daryl thinks it would be a distraction. Plus, I wouldn't want to make things hard for you."

"It's okay," Hailey said. "I'm going to call him. Probably tomorrow."

The words sounded far hollow to her own ears now that she said them out loud.

"Do you think Caleb would want to be part of Ferris's life?" Phoebe asked.

Renee's eyes flitted to the goody basket. Then she leaned over, grabbed a bag of popcorn and opened it noisily.

"Forget what Caleb wants," Renee said, pointedly, and her voice rose. She jabbed her index finger through the air at Hailey to punctuate her words. "This is about you and what you want. Do you want to tell Ferris that his dad is a police officer named Caleb with a K-9 dog?"

Okay, but Hailey didn't see what Caleb's career or Sheb had to do with—

Before she could even complete the thought, she heard a sudden crash and clatter.

She turned. Ferris was standing behind her, a metal bowl at his feet as a smattering of nuts, chocolate-covered fruits and other rejected snacks skittered across the floor around him. Her son's blue eyes were wide. Hailey's heart stuttered.

Why hadn't any of them noticed Ferris was there?

What had he overheard?

FOUR

She'd have never wanted him to find out this way. She'd always thought she'd have more time before Ferris started asking questions, and that maybe by then she'd have worked out how to include Caleb in the conversation. But now her friend's thoughtfulness had snatched the choice out of her hands.

"Oops, I'm so sorry..." Renee's apologetic voice came from somewhere behind her.

She could also hear the faint sound of Phoebe praying for her.

But Hailey didn't turn. Instead, she crouched down until she was eye level with her son.

"Hi, sweetie! Let's get these cleaned up." She quickly scooped the spilled treats back up and dumped them in the bowl. Her heart ached to see that charming and impish smile that would tell her everything okay. Normally, Ferris would've been quick to leap in to help. Instead, he looked as shocked and startled as he had the first time he'd seen fireworks. "Is everything okay? Did you hear some of what the adults were talking about?"

He nodded and when he spoke, his voice was barely above an awed whisper. "Does my dad really have a police dog?"

Half laugh and half sob slipped past her lips.

"Yes," she admitted. "Your daddy is policeman with a dog."

A bright smile spread like a sunrise across his face. "I like dogs!"

Before she could answer, a pattering of footsteps and a chorus of voices clamored down the hallway toward them. Phoebe's five-year-old twins, River and Lake, and Renee's three-year-old son, Fisher, charged into the kitchen to all announce at once that the cartoons they'd been watching had stopped and they wanted more snacks.

"Mom, did you see the big candy basket?" Ferris asked, the police dog and his absent father apparently forgotten. At least for the moment.

"I did!" Hailey scooped him up into an embrace and he wrapped his arms around her neck. "Auntie Phoebe said we can even take some home. But you and I are not going to have any more now or we'll both spoil our appetites for dinner."

To her surprise, the end of her sentence was almost swallowed up by a sudden yawn, as an unexpected wave of fatigue swept over her body. She hadn't realized how tired she was. Her cheeks felt hot and flushed too. Then again, she'd had more than enough emotional upheaval for one day.

And I might fall into a sugar coma. Renee and her children decided to head out then as well. Her friend whispered a few more quick apologies under her breath as they wrangled the kids, and Hailey reassured her it was okay. After all, she'd prayed that God would guide the timing of all this. Now, she'd just have to keep praying that God would keep guiding her—and Caleb—whatever happened next.

Phoebe loaded up bags of goodies and pressed them into Hailey's and Renee's hands. There were rounds of hugs goodbye, a flurry of tiny feet wriggling into shoes, and repeated reminders of when they'd be meeting up for the final dress fittings and the wedding rehearsal later that week.

Then Hailey buckled Ferris into his booster in the back seat, got in the driver's seat and started for home. The sun was sitting low in the spring sky and seemed to be blazing straight into her eyes at every turn, no matter how much she fiddled with the sun visor. Her skin was still warm and her eyelids drooped. She rolled the window down and let the breeze cool her face.

"Did you have fun?" she asked. She could always count on her friend to watch Ferris when she was at work.

"Yes!" he exclaimed, emphatically. She pulled to a stop at a red light and glanced back at her son in the rearview mirror. His smile beamed. "We practiced being bears!"

He raised his hands above him like claws and roared loudly. She laughed and turned back to the light, in time to watch it turn green. Thankfully, he'd still forgotten about his dad being a police officer and having a dog for now, but the knowledge of what her son now knew ticked at the edge of her consciousness like a bomb waiting to explode when she least expected. Her stomach was a bit unsettled now, maybe due to wolfing down that much sugar back at Phoebe's. Ferris kept roaring.

"Bears?" she asked.

"Yes, because me an' River an' Fisher are gonna be ring bears for Auntie Phoebe's wedding!"

Phoebe had included both her and Renee's children in the wedding party, along with her own.

"Ring bearers means ring carriers," she said. "It means you have the important job of carrying Auntie Phoebe's and Uncle Daryl's rings."

Her son frowned. "How many rings?"

"Two."

"Are they big and heavy?"

"No, they're very little."

"Oh." Ferris sounded deflated.

"But they'll probably be in a box."

"A big box?" her son asked, hopefully.

"Maybe," she said. Hailey blinked. Her eyes felt dry and tired, probably a lingering effect of the smoke. Her stomach had gone from sour to queasy. Well, they'd be home soon enough and then she could catnap on the couch while dinner was in the oven. "We'll find out what Auntie Phoebe has planned on Friday at the rehearsal."

"They'll be very big," Ferris declared, confidently.

Then he went back to roaring. She laughed again and felt her heart surge with love for the impetuous little guy in the back seat.

Lord, thank You so much for my son. He is a gift and a blessing from You and he gives me far more joy than I ever imagined.

And she was pretty sure God was now asking her to share him with Caleb, no matter how much she might slightly and protectively want to pretend otherwise. Secretly, some nights she lay awake imagining scenarios where she confronted Caleb about Ferris, and Caleb immediately offered to give up paternity, saying he wanted nothing to do with the boy. Somehow, that was less scary than having to figure out how to co-parent her amazing little kid with a man who worked on a police force fifteen hours away. How would that even work? She was never going to move Ferris to Toronto, and Caleb was never going to move home to Thunder Bay. Surely, Ferris was better off with no father at all than one who was part-time and reluctant. At least, that was what she told herself. Of course, in her dream scenario there was also always some handsome, kind, faithful, loving and perfect man waiting in the wings, who wanted to step in and help her as Ferris grew up.

Lord, I'll be obedient to you. But please, don't let Caleb hurt Ferris's heart!

Mighty roars erupted from the back seat again.

She laughed and then yawned again. Sun shone bright off the hood of her small yellow car. Forest and rock were flying past her window now, with a glimpse of dark blue waters through the trees. She blinked. She'd been so distracted and tired, she'd gotten turned around and taken the road out of town at the previous traffic light, when she should have headed downtown into the city. Okay, so now she needed to find a place to stop and turn around…

Hailey's eyes drifted shut. She blinked again, jolting back hard in her seat.

She'd almost fallen asleep at the wheel.

Help me, Lord…

Something was wrong. Was she sick?

She didn't think the paramedics had given her any drugs or other medication….

She nodded off again and shook herself back awake. Her heart raced into her throat. She was on a one-lane country road now. A transport truck blared its horn and swerved around her, so closely her windows rattled. Her fingers felt like they were slipping off the wheel. She didn't even recognize the road she was on! Hailey had always enjoyed taking unexpected turns and routes home—but not like this.

She slowed down. She had to stop. She had to get off the road. Desperately, she searched the road ahead for anywhere safe she could pull over. But the road was narrow, with tight curves and tall trees. Her vision was blurry. She didn't want to crash or risk stopping somewhere they might get hit by an oncoming car.

The basket full of drinks and candy filled her mind. Had her drink been spiked? Had she been drugged? Was this how Matty had felt before he crashed his car and died? His emotional state had seemed a bit loopy that night. But if she was drugged, then how? The paramedics had given her a bottle of water after the bank robbery. Had one of the Goats or one of their accomplices slipped something into it? Or had something she'd eaten or drank at Phoebe's been drugged? In which case, she might not have been the target—and her friends and their kids might also be in danger. But all her thoughts seemed to churn inside her mind like clothes in a washing machine, and she could barely grab hold of any one of them long enough to see it clearly.

As she tried to pray, one fear shone huge and bright above them all.

If she lost control of her car right now, she might kill her son.

God please, please protect my Ferris...

Ferris was now singing to himself. It was the theme song of his favorite television show about a brave little police dog. Was he thinking about what he'd learned about Caleb? Hailey held on to the sound of her son's voice and used it to battle against whatever this illness was that surged through her body and tried to drag her down. The road was rough dirt and gravel beneath her tires. Somehow, she'd missed a turn and was now on an unpaved road she didn't even recognize. Hang on, wasn't this near the rocks where she and Caleb had shared their first kiss? What was she doing here? A boat launch lay ahead. She aimed for it. Her heartbeat seemed to be pounding through her skull, sending black spots before her eyes.

She wasn't going to make it.

Dial 911... Phone, dial 911...

She tried to say it but the words wouldn't come out.

She swerved off the highway toward the boat launch.

"Mommy? Are you okay?"

No, Mommy's very sleepy.

Her wheel hit the edge of the curb then rolled down toward the water. She tried to press her foot against the brake, but it was like her limbs were made of jelly.

Sudden ringing filled the car. She glanced at the cell phone mounted on her dashboard.

The screen read Caleb.

"Caleb!" Ferris exclaimed. Her son had read it too. "Is my daddy calling?!"

Yes.

"Answer the phone, Mommy!" Ferris shouted. "Answer the phone!"

But it was too late to tell him that now.

It was too late to tell him anything.

Because the drowsiness had won. Her feet couldn't press the brakes.

Her car was rolling into the water.

Her eyes closed.

"Mommy!" Ferris's voice rose. "Mommy! Wake up! We're sinking!"

But she couldn't answer him.

Please, save him, Lord...

"Answer call!" Ferris shouted at her cell phone, like he'd heard her say countless times before. "Phone, answer call! Get my police daddy!"

"Hello?" Caleb's voice filled the car.

"Daddy!" Ferris's shouts filled her mind as unconsciousness finally took her over and dragged her under. "Daddy Policeman, please help us!"

* * *

Caleb had no idea what was happening on the other end of the phone. All he really could really hear was a high-pitched yell followed by the faint sound of something crashing. For all he knew, Hailey had seen his name on the phone, screeched in annoyance and tossed it across the room. Caleb clenched his hands around the steering wheel and merged his truck onto the highway.

"I don't want to fight. I just wanted to tell you I was leaving town now, but of course I'll help with the bank heist investigation into the Goats in any—"

"Help!" The faint and plaintive echoing of what sounded like a child's screams reached his ears through the phone. "Help me!"

Caleb's heart stopped as immediately, instinctively, he eased his foot off the gas and pulled onto the side of the highway. Sheb growled from the back seat, and he signaled the K-9 to be quiet.

"Hello?" Caleb called. He pushed the volume up as he racked his memory for Hailey's son's name. "Ferris? Are you okay?"

"We need help!" A boy's voice filled the cab. "The car's getting wet!"

Wet?

"Ferris?" Caleb's heart began to race. "Where are you?"

"In the wet car," Ferris called.

"Like a car wash?"

"Nuh-uh."

Right, he was trying to get important information from a four-year-old.

"Where's your mom?" Caleb asked.

"She's asleep."

"Can you wake her up for me?"

"Nuh-uh. She's too asleep."

Caleb's heart beat faster. Did that mean she was unconscious? Injured? Whatever that meant it did not sound good. But what mattered now was figuring out where they were and sending help. Vehicles honked as they raced past him on the highway.

"Where is the car right now?" Caleb tried again.

"In the lake!" Ferris shouted. "We crashed!"

They'd crashed into Lake Superior?

The banks were steep and the water could be fierce. Not to mention, it was the largest freshwater lake in the world. Depending on where they'd crashed, the water could quickly swallow them whole.

An ugly memory filled his mind, unbidden, of Matty's car buried in its murky depths, with his cousin slumped dead behind the wheel.

"Help us! Daddy Policeman!"

"Just hang tight," Caleb said, without bothering to correct him. Didn't matter what the kid called him for now— all that mattered was keeping Ferris calm and making sure he was okay. "You and your mom are going to be okay. I promise. I'm going to get the police to find you."

His mind spun. Did this have anything to do with the Goats and the attack at the bank? What would he even tell 911? A car had crashed somewhere in the water with an unconscious woman and child inside? But where? Presumably somewhere shallow, considering they hadn't sunk too quickly. Still, there were over thirty-five miles of local coast to cover, not to mention dozens of inlets and coves. Thick tree cover, dense forest and jagged rocks would hamper air, land and water searches. All he could really tell dispatch right now was that they needed to find a single, urgent needle in miles and miles of haystacks.

Guide me, Lord.

"I'm going to put you on hold for one moment," Caleb said, "just so I can call 911. It'll sound like I'm gone, but I promise I'll be back."

"No, no! Please, no! Don't do a hold! Stay!" Ferris squealed. A crunch sounded through the phone. "I need you to come help us, Daddy!"

If the call did disconnect, would Caleb be able to reconnect? If there was even a fraction of chance that putting Ferris on hold would drop the call and terrify the child further, it was a chance he wasn't about to take.

Suddenly, it was like a breaker switch flipped inside Caleb's chest. If Ferris was Matty's son, he was family, and Caleb should've stepped up long ago to be the kind father figure Matty would've been and wanted him to be. After all, if the roles had been reversed, wouldn't Matty have done everything his power to step up and help raise Caleb's child? "I won't put you on hold. I promise. I'm going to stay right here with you on the phone until you and your mommy are okay."

Lord, please help me find them and keep Ferris calm.

Caleb shot a quick glance at the mirrors, yanked the wheel hard to the left and gunned the engine, throwing the vehicle into a sharp, tight U-turn. At the same time, he quickly punched the three-digit code into his dashboard-mounted phone that would summon all available members of the Cold Case Task Force onto an emergency group call. They could coordinate rescue with emergency services, patch into his car's GPS and feed all necessary information to dispatchers, while he just focused on keeping Ferris calm.

"Hold on, I'm coming!"

An icon appeared on his phone telling him that Gemma

was in the process of answering. According to the screen, Lucas Harper in the task force main office and Blake Murphy, the team's Ontario Provincial Police liaison, were logging in to the call now too. A junction loomed ahead. Should he take the main road or small one? He breathed and prayed and chose the rural road that cut closer to the shoreline. Sheb barked.

"Is that your police dog puppy?" Ferris asked.

"Sure is," Caleb said.

"I like dogs," Ferris said. Bravery seemed to battle the fear in the little boy's voice. "What's his name?"

"Sheb."

"Sheb is a silly name," Ferris said.

"I think so too!" Gemma's voice joined the call. It was the same bright and cheerful tone she used when talking to Jackson's little girl, Skye, yet Caleb could hear the tense and worried edge cutting through her words. "Is this Ferris? I'm Caleb's friend Gemma, and I'm here to help."

"We need you to call emergency services and dispatch search and rescue to find Hailey Blue's car," Caleb said.

"We smashed and now we're in the water!" Ferris interrupted.

"Oh no," Gemma said, and the sound of typing came down the line. He could tell she was battling to keep her tone level. "Their car is in Lake Superior. We need everyone to work together very, very fast to find them."

He heard more typing and could only guess what all was going on behind the scenes that he couldn't hear. Jackson was on the call now and their boss Finnick too. The only member who hadn't shown up was Oscar—the mysterious, unknown member of the team who was on a long-running undercover mission. None of them had ever met him, but Finnick trusted him implicitly.

"Are you in your mommy's yellow car?" Gemma asked.

"Yes!" Ferris said, quickly and eager to help. "It's like a banana!"

"A banana car," Gemma said, "got it."

Immediately, Caleb's phone pinged with confirmation from Gemma that the team had already identified Hailey's vehicle's make, model and license plate, followed by the reassurance that 911, search and rescue, and provincial police had now all been contacted and were mobilizing a large-scale search. They were also checking traffic cameras and with friends to narrow down where they might have gone.

Relief filled his chest. *Thank You, God.*

"You said your mommy fell asleep," Gemma said, gently. "Was it all at once? Or very slowly?"

"I don't know." Ferris sounded circumspect. "I didn't notice. I was singing. She was driving funny though."

"Funny how?" Caleb asked.

"Like a ride!" Ferris said. "Whee! Swoosh!"

So, maybe she'd slowly lost control. Drugs seemed more likely. Matty had been found with a lethal dose of sleeping pills in his system. Had the same thing happened to her? Rocks and trees flashed past his truck. He tried to focus on the thought of his coworkers and teammates, scattered around at their desks, all doing their part, furiously coordinating the search and rescue effort with law enforcement.

Caleb could only hope that Hailey was still breathing. Despite Gemma's reassurance that search and rescue had been deployed, Caleb couldn't hear so much as a siren or see a helicopter in the air or a flashing light on the horizon. Were they even searching in the right place? Was he going in the right direction?

"Hurry up!" Ferris's called. "The water's getting closer!"

"We are," Gemma reassured him.

Messages from Gemma continued to pop up on Caleb's phone. Apparently, Hailey hadn't taken the expected route home. At least, they couldn't find her passing the traffic lights they'd have expected her to.

"How about we play a police question game?" Caleb suggested. "I'll say some things, and you tell me if you can see them. Okay?"

"Okay!" The little boy sounded so hopeful. Caleb prayed they wouldn't let him and Hailey down.

According to Ferris, he could see trees, water and islands. But no matter how the little boy twisted and turned in his seat, he could not see a road, which was a really bad sign, because it meant people driving along the road might not see them.

"Ferris, can you see a lighthouse?" Gemma asked.

"No," Ferris said, and Caleb could almost hear him shaking his head.

Okay, so they weren't in view of the Welcome Islands or any of the other half dozen lighthouses that marked the shoreline.

"Any buildings at all?" Gemma pressed.

"No! Please hurry!"

The road ahead curved away from the water. A private unmarked road lay to the left. A thought crossed Caleb's mind. Hailey had never been one to take the expected route anywhere. When they were younger, she'd wander down unmarked roads and off beaten paths, as if she enjoyed the adventure of getting lost and trying to find her way home. He still remembered the first time she'd taken him for a random drive. That'd been the day they'd had their first kiss. Maybe instead of defaulting to the expected routes, she'd driven somewhere unexpected? She'd likely been drugged or injured. Her brain had been addled.

"Ferris, was the road bumpy before you crashed?" Caleb asked.

There was a pause. Then Ferris said, "Yes! Super bumpy!"

Caleb whispered a prayer and steered onto the smaller unpaved road. The truck shook and jolted as the tires kicked up gravel. Sheb woofed from the back seat. An even narrower road split off ahead; again, Caleb veered onto the smaller and more obscure road, instead of taking the tighter turn, which would keep him on a main road. He was following a hunch. One he couldn't put into words. The water was shallow here, which matched the fact that the car was still partially above water. Jagged rocks jutted out of the water.

"Ferris," he said, "I have a very important question for you. Do the islands you can see have lots of trees?"

"Nuh-uh," Ferris said. "They look like rock blocks in a bathtub."

Rock blocks in a bathtub. Yeah, not a bad description for what Caleb could see now.

"Gemma, do you have my location on GPS right now?" Caleb asked.

"Yeah, I do," Gemma said. "But you're still nowhere near the search radius."

Probably because every time he'd reached a fork in the road he'd taken the less obvious one. Just like Hailey used to do. She'd said it made life more interesting.

The tree cover was so thick he could only catch fleeting glimpses of the water. He slowed the car down to a crawl and inched forward. *God, please help me see.* Then he saw it. A bright flash of yellow shone against brilliant blue water in between the green wall of trees. His chest tightened as if he was afraid to breathe, let alone hope.

A boat launch sign loomed ahead. He pulled toward it.

Sheb sniffed the air then woofed softly. A heartbeat later, the trees finally parted, the water came into view and now he could see Hailey's car.

"I found it!" He hit the brakes, grabbed his phone off the dashboard, leaped out and ran toward the water, with Sheb at his heels. The car was titled precariously in the lake, several feet away from the shore. The water had already almost completely swallowed the hood and the vehicle was still rolling deeper into the water.

"Daddy! Daddy, I see you!" Ferris shouted down the line and Caleb could see him bouncing up and down in the back seat and waving his arms through the rear window.

"We see you too!" He kicked off his boots as he ran toward the water. Sheb howled as the K-9 sprinted beside him. "Gemma, I'm going in!"

FIVE

"I've got your location!" Gemma said. "Sending rescue your way!"

"Thanks!" He toed off his shoes then pulled his jacket off and dropped it on the ground. "See you on the other side."

He threw his phone down onto his jacket and leaped into the water.

"Sheb!" he ordered. "Stay!"

Sheb woofed loudly but stayed on the shore. The ground was muddy and slick under Caleb's feet. He sunk in the muck up to his ankles. Thick seaweed wrapped around his legs. But he focused his eyes on the car ahead and pushed forward. He reached the car. The water was up to his shoulders now.

Ferris still bounced, waved and shouted in the back seat. Hailey lay slumped over the steering wheel. There was no way to carry them both to shore at once. Caleb grabbed the back door handle and yanked it so hard that he practically snapped his fingers back when it turned out to be locked.

"Ferris!" Caleb turned to the child. "I need you to unlock the door."

"Can I undo my seat belt first?" Ferris called.

"Yes!"

The four-year-old's face filled the window as he reached for the door and fiddled with the lock. Caleb and Ferris were nose to nose, their faces only divided by the pane of glass and for the very first time, Caleb saw the boy's face. His heart lurched hard. Truth was, although Caleb had never seen Ferris in person and had avoided all photos of the child, he'd always carried a very specific mental image of Ferris in his mind. He'd pictured the boy as a mini Matty, with a mop of dark curly hair and mischievous brown eyes. Instead, Caleb stared through the window at a blond, tousled-haired tyke who was almost the spitting image of Caleb at that age. His heart stopped.

He's a mini me.

Ferris grabbed the door handle; Caleb grabbed it too and together they yanked it open. Water gushed in, filling the car and instantly plunging it deeper into the water. Ferris's face paled in fear as the waters suddenly rose around him. The boy tried to leap into Caleb's open arms, only to lose his footing and fall. But Caleb was there to catch him. He bundled Ferris into his arms. Ferris clutched him back so tightly he almost choked. The boy shuddered a sob and Caleb ran a protective hand down his neck.

"I got you." Caleb turned and ran through the water back toward the shore. "You're safe."

"No wait!" Ferris yelled. "You need to get my mommy too!"

Panic filled the boy's voice. Tears flooded his little eyes.

"I will!" Caleb's heart broke. "I'm just going to take you to shore first."

But the boy kept yelling "no" as if he was afraid that if Caleb didn't grab Hailey now he'd never see her again.

"It's okay, it's okay," he reassured the boy softly, holding him tightly, even as the kid began to wriggle and fight in his arms.

Sheb was waiting for them, barking nervously and dancing his paws in and out of the water. Caleb knelt down in the mud, and the K-9 began to nuzzle Ferris with his snout.

"Stay here with Sheb," Caleb said, gently but firmly. "I'm going to go back and get your mom."

Ferris was still shaking his head, but Caleb eased the boy's hands from around his neck. For a second he was afraid the child was going to grab him again, but instead Ferris wrapped his arms around Sheb and hugged him tightly. The Belgian Malinois started to lick the boy's face.

Good dog.

Caleb thanked God silently for his partner and dashed back into the water, praying hard with every step. The car was sinking faster now. Caleb pushed himself through the muck, helplessly watching as the car tipped forward, nose first and then sunk deeper and deeper.

Help me, Lord!

He had to rescue Hailey. He had to get her out of there.

He'd wasted so many years being angry and resenting her. Now, he'd give anything to know she was safe. The car vanished completely.

Caleb took a deep breath and dove for her. For a moment, he couldn't see anything but a wall of murky green gray. Then he found the door, pushed his way through and reached Hailey. She was still unconscious. Her blond hair streamed around her. And Caleb realized he was praying harder for her survival than he ever had for anything in his life. His fingers fumbled for her seat belt. He pulled her out of the car, cradled her to his chest and swam for the surface. Moments later, he could feel the ground under his feet again. He was vaguely aware that the world around him had suddenly erupted in sirens and flashing lights. Emergency vehicles swarmed the road. Helicopter blades roared ahead. People in uniform rushed toward them. But as he stumbled through the water toward the shore, all he could see was the bright smile on Ferris's face and the soft features of the woman now lying safe against his chest.

He brushed the blond strands off Hailey's neck and felt for a pulse. She coughed. Her eyes fluttered open. For a moment, their blue-green depths searched his face. His heart began to beat again.

"Caleb…" His name left her lips as a whisper. Her head fell against him.

He opened his mouth and tried to respond, only to find a thick lump in his throat.

Paramedics splashed through the water toward them, then carefully took Hailey from his arms and rushed her to the ambulance. For a moment, he stood there in the knee-deep water, watching her go.

Then he saw Ferris and Sheb running around the shoreline toward him, with a worried paramedic dashing after him, trying to catch up with the excited boy.

Caleb ran for Ferris, swept him up into his arms and then nodded to the paramedic.

"You got her!" Ferris said.

"I did," Caleb said. "Now come on, we're going to let this nice paramedic take a look at us, get in an ambulance and go to the hospital for your mommy to get checked out."

Ferris hugged him deeply. "I knew you could do it, Daddy!"

Daddy?

Was he really this boy's father? Caleb hugged him back. The lump grew thicker.

Lord, what do I do now?

* * *

Hailey was dreaming and she couldn't wake up. At least not fully. Instead, it was like she kept coming close to the surface of her consciousness, before plunging back down into the depths of sleep again. Disjointed thoughts and feelings seemed to fly around her like she was caught inside a tornadic waterspout, and she couldn't grab a hold of any of them long enough to make sense of what was happening. Ferris was roaring like a bear and singing. She was driving her car through the woods and underwater.

Then somehow she was in Caleb's arms and he was holding her.

And she knew she was safe.

Slowly, sounds and sensations came into focus around her. A soft mattress lay beneath her back and warm, dry blankets enveloped her body. Bright fluorescent lights shone on her closed eyelids. Her right arm was itchy and seemed to be attached to something. A machine beeped rhythmically. Her eyelids fluttered but felt too heavy to open. Voices murmured at the edges of her consciousness, indistinct at first but then slowly coming into focus.

"Here I go superfast...*vroom vroom*..." It was Ferris. Her son's voice was coming from somewhere on the other side of the room. Her heart warmed to the sound. "Whee... *screech*..."

Her son was playing cars. She could hear the faint sound of metal wheels skittering across a tiled floor.

"Here comes a police car," a warm and deep male voice chimed in the game. *"Whee-whoo whee-whoo..."*

She felt her eyelids flutter again. She knew that voice. But for a moment she couldn't grab hold of the face and name that went with it.

"Oh no!" Ferris squealed with laughter. "Go faster... faster...*zoooom*!"

Hailey heard the car roll across the room and crash into something. Ferris dissolved in a fit of giggles. The man laughed too. Her heart beat quickened. No matter how long she lived, she'd never forget how much she loved hearing that sound...

"Caleb..."

She opened her eyes and pushed back against the pillows, then struggled to sit. She was in a small hospital room. The sky was dark outside the window, and there was IV was in her arm and bright lights overhead. She was wearing a gray tracksuit that she recognized as the kind search and rescue provided to people in emergencies. At first, the only people she saw was the male nurse talking to a uniformed cop that stood by the door.

"Mommy!" Ferris shouted, excitedly. "Mommy, you're awake!"

Only then did she look down over the side of the bed, just in time to see Ferris leaping up off the floor, where he'd apparently been playing cars with Caleb and his puppy, Sheb. Her son was wearing similar track pants and a cheerful green Amethyst Harbour T-shirt she recognized from the hospital gift shop. Caleb was wearing a matching shirt and mud-streaked jeans. What had happened to them all? She spread her arms as best as she could as Ferris launched himself into her embrace and hugged her tightly.

"See, Daddy!" he called. "Mommy's all better?"

Daddy?

A sharp pain filled her chest as if hearing her son say the word was somehow physically squeezing her heart. She looked over the top of her son's head at Caleb, searching his face for answers.

Had Caleb told her son to call him that?

Why would he ever do something like that?

But the blue eyes that stared back into hers, over their son's head, were so calm and distant, almost emotionless.

"He wanted to do crafts," Caleb said. "But all the hospital had were cars. Your son is a really amazing kid."

Before she could figure out what to say to that, Caleb turned, stepped away from the bed and went to talk to the cop by the door. The nurse came over, checked on Hailey's vitals, asked her a few questions about how she was doing, and told her that the doctor would come and give her answers when he could. Ferris talked the whole time, telling her a long story about the lake, the car, Caleb and Sheb, that she could barely make heads or tails off.

Questions crowded her mind so quickly she could barely breathe. But she didn't want to ask any of them with Ferris in the room. As long as law enforcement and medical staff were letting her take the time to hug and reassure her son, then presumably whatever they had to tell her about what had happened could wait. Then again, there was still a cop at her hospital door.

A grandmotherly nurse she knew from church appeared and gently ushered Ferris out with the promise of cookies and Jell-O. The other nurse left the room too, and the cop stepped away from the door. Suddenly, Hailey was alone, except for where Caleb stood silent, propping the door open with his leg and just one step away from disappearing out into the hall, as well. Caleb looked down at this phone and seemed to be texting someone.

"Why did Ferris call you Daddy?" she asked.

"I honestly don't know," Caleb said. He pocketed his phone. "But arguing with him about it didn't seem like the right thing to do."

That didn't answer her question. She opened her mouth, but he went on before she could figure out what to say.

"I'm glad you're doing okay," Caleb went on, without really meeting her eyes. "My dad's on his way with a couple of cops to question you about what happened. But don't worry. You're out of the woods. Ferris is fine and no one else was injured."

"Wait!" She sat up as far as she could, then realized she'd done it too fast. "Don't go. I want to talk."

"Don't move like that." Worry and annoyance flashed across his face as he rushed across the room, letting the door swing shut behind him. "You'll pull out your IV."

He reached for her, as if to push her back down, then hesitated. Instead, she grabbed both his hands in hers. Or at least she tried to. He pulled away immediately, so that all she grabbed were his sleeves.

"Please talk to me," she said. "It's all a blur. I'm scared, I'm confused and I don't know what happened."

"Fine." He nodded and crossed his arms in front of his chest. She recognized his stance. He was in cop mode. Just the facts. No emotion. As if she was nothing but another person he was briefing in the line of duty. "What's the last thing you remember?"

She paused. Now that was a good question. She wasn't exactly sure.

"We were leaving Phoebe's house," she said, slowly. "I remember feeling sleepy—" She gasped and felt her eyes widen. "Did I crash? Was Ferris hurt?"

"I told you, he's fine." Caleb cast a glance toward the door as if hoping someone would appear who'd save him from the conversation. No one did. He looked back at her, and this time she noted a little more warmth in his gaze.

"Phoebe received a large gift basket at the house. It was supposedly from the wedding rehearsal venue, but police haven't confirmed where it came from yet. Two of the drinks were dosed with high levels of sedatives. Both grapefruit. You drank from one of them and passed out. CSI found them in your car and tested them."

Her lips parted again and he held up a hand before she could continue. "And yes, Ferris, Phoebe, Renee and all the kids are fine—everybody is fine. Paramedics tested all of them too. You were the only person who was affected."

She exhaled. "Thank God for that."

For a moment, she almost thought she caught the faintest glimmer of a smile curl at the edges of his lips, but it disappeared so fast she wondered if she'd only imagined it.

"Did it have anything to do with the Goats or the bank heist?" she asked.

"Not that we know of," Caleb said. "But I've never been a big fan of coincidences."

Neither had she. But that also didn't mean they were impossible.

"Why were only the grapefruit ones drugged?" she asked.

"Beats me." He shrugged. "Maybe they were the only ones with a strong enough taste to hide the drugs."

So, had it been another coincidence that she'd been the only one who liked that flavor?

"Where did I pass out?"

"In your car." Caleb sounded tired. "In the lake."

"Like Matty—" The words slipped out as quietly as a whisper.

"Exactly like Matty." Caleb nodded. "Sleeping pills, followed by a car crash in Lake Superior. It was even the exact same brand of sleeping pills too. But, unlike Matty, we found you in time."

He sat down on the edge of her bed. Sheb laid his head on the bed beside him. He ran his hand over the dog's ears.

"I was on my way out of town," he went on. "I felt this strong nudge to call you. Ferris answered the phone and filled me in."

Her mind boggled. Her brave and plucky four-year-old had somehow coordinated their rescue?

"I messaged my team," Caleb said. "They called search and rescue. I stayed on the phone with Ferris and he helped me find you."

Her mind still spun trying to catch up with everything he was telling her. Ferris must've been so scared, and to think that when she'd woken up, he'd been laughing and happily playing cars.

"You took really good care of him," she said. She could feel something like awe slipping through her words as a feeling she couldn't explain warmed in her chest.

"Yeah, well, he'd a good kid." Caleb stood again. "Anyway, I'm sure the doctor will come fill you in on all the medical particulars soon. Your dose was low—barely a quarter of drugs in the can—and we found you before it was too late. They flushed out your system, got you rehydrated and let you sleep it off. You've been in and out of consciousness for a while, but nothing they were worried about. Anyway, I've told you everything we know as far as the investigation goes. For now, we assume that Phoebe was the intended target. I'm sure my dad's going to have his best cops on it, and of course my team will assist in any way we can."

He turned toward the door. But she reached out again and touched his arm.

"Should we talk more about the fact you let Ferris call you Daddy?" she asked.

Did that mean he was open to being part of her son's life? Did that mean he was ready to step up and be Ferris's dad?

He spun back, and for the first time since she'd woken up she saw the full force of the emotion he'd apparently been keeping at bay sweep across his face. His jaw clenched. His eyes flashed.

Caleb was angry. At her? At himself? Probably at both of them.

"I told you," Caleb said. "He started calling me that on the phone and I didn't respond to it, one way or the other. Keeping him safe and calm, and finding you guys was my top priority. And if that's created a mess for you, I'm sorry, but I guess we're just going to have to figure that out tomorrow. In the meantime, we both need to rest."

"Does that mean you believe me now, about Ferris being your son?"

His gaze focused on her face. "Look me in the eyes and tell me Ferris is my son."

"Ferris is your son," Hailey said, feeling an unexpected sob slip through the words. "You're the only man who could possibly be his father and I'm happy to take a DNA test, if you still don't believe me."

For a long moment he held her gaze. Then he looked away.

"I believe you," Caleb said. "Then again, he is the spitting image of me." He turned toward the door again and something hardened in his voice. "But I also don't know what to think. I don't like how you handled this, but I don't exactly have the high ground now, do I?"

Hot tears sprang to her eyes. "I'm sorry."

"Oh, me too."

Before she had to worry about whether she'd let her tears fall in front of him, he shoved his shoulder into the door and walked out into the hall, with Sheb by his side. The door swung shut behind him.

SIX

He had a son. A bright, smart, brave and amazing little boy—and Caleb had missed the first four years of his life completely. And why? Because he'd believed Matty would never lie to him? Because he'd been so convinced that Hailey was lying? Because the sense of bitterness that had swept over him all those years ago—not just from losing Hailey but from losing his best friend in such a tragic and unexpected way—had settled in his heart and mind like a stubborn fog that might never lift? Any man would be overjoyed to discover he had a son like Ferris, but instead, right now all he could feel was a cyclone of guilt, anger and confusion, swirling so fast inside him that it hurt to breathe.

He didn't mean to kick the garbage next to him, but he did and it tipped over. But of course, any momentary and fleeting satisfaction he might've felt in taking out how he felt about himself on an inanimate object vanished when he looked up to see his father appearing around the corner, flanked by a doctor and two armed officers. Police Chief Sylvester Perry glanced from the spilled garbage to his son's face and raised an eyebrow. Heat rose to the back of Caleb's neck. He bent down and scooped the garbage back into the can.

"Everything okay?" his dad asked. While Sylvester

stopped, the others kept walking down the hall and entered Hailey's room. "I heard Hailey's doing well."

"Yeah." Caleb stood and set the garbage can upright. Sheb sat neatly and wagged his tail. "Her memory is foggy but I filled her in quickly about what happened and what we know." He ran his hands down his mostly-dry-but-muddy jeans. He'd ridden to the hospital in the ambulance with Ferris, and the hospital hadn't had a pair of pants available in his size, besides scrubs. "Anything new on the case?"

"No," his dad said, and frowned. "Sedatives were over-the-counter medication. Looks like somebody crushed them into a fine powder and then drugged the drinks by piercing them with a needle. It would all definitely take some work but not rocket science. We haven't been able to confirm with the reception venue that they sent the basket. So, who knows who sent it or why."

"Do you think they were after Phoebe?" Caleb asked. "It's eerily similar to how Matty died."

"Your guess is as good as mine." Sylvester shook his head and shrugged.

"And the sleeping pills that Hailey was drugged with are the exact same ones that Matty was, right?" Caleb confirmed. "Same brand and everything?"

"I'm afraid so." His father nodded.

Caleb took a deep breath and summoned the courage to ask the question he knew he should've asked years ago. "Where are you at in investigating Matty's murder?"

"It's still an open and active investigation," his dad said, "but it's fair to say it's been slow-moving. We've taken witness statements from all staff and guests who were at the wedding Matty attended before he died—over three hundred people in total—as well as statements from the patrons at the diner he met with Hailey at before he died.

But we've yet to uncover a motive for his murder or how he was drugged."

The police chief spoke slowly, as if carefully measuring his words.

Caleb nodded. Some cases took a very long time to solve, which is why it usually took ten years before a case was considered cold.

"Did the Goats ever drug anyone?" Caleb asked.

He fully expected the answer to be no.

Instead his dad said, "Possibly. Certainly the public think so. It appears that in the first robbery they might've slipped something into a security guard's soup, which made him sick. But by the time somebody thought to test his takeaway bowl and blood, it was too late to trace anything. Then in the second they piped carbon monoxide into the ventilation system."

"So, word on the street is that the Goats have drugged people, but you're not about to speculate without hard evidence?"

His father smiled. "Exactly."

Huh. Caleb knew his dad well enough to know that was the only answer he was likely to get, until his dad had something solid. His dad had never been one for guesswork. Not like Caleb's teammates, who were constantly turning to each other to brainstorm when things were rough—whether personal or professional. And right now, Caleb was struggling with both.

He needed someone to bounce ideas off of.

"Also, before today none of the Goats robberies have fallen within my jurisdiction," his father added. "Now that one has, I'm coordinating out efforts with the police chief in Thunder Bay."

"Anything new on the bank heist?" Caleb asked.

"Nothing," his dad said. "Our two killers knew the area well enough to avoid being caught by either cameras or witnesses without their masks on. Your mom wants you to call her."

"I will," Caleb said, "although honestly I'm afraid she'll start trying to give me her opinion about Hailey and Ferris, and that's the last thing I need right now."

"You could always tell her that," his dad said.

Then before Caleb could find an answer to that, Chief Perry continued down the hall toward Hailey's room. Caleb and Sheb started back toward the lobby. There was a line of people waiting for the elevator, so he took to the stairs. His heart was still pounding. His head was still churning.

He needed to talk this out.

He pulled his phone before he'd made it down half a flight of stairs and called Jackson and Gemma. The sound of the phone ringing seemed to echo through the stairwell.

"Hello?" Jackson was on the line.

"Hey," Caleb said.

"Do Gemma a favor and cancel her from the call," Jackson said. "She's downstairs packing like a whirlwind, but she'll beat herself up for not being there for you. Unless this is urgent?"

"No," Caleb said. "I just needed to let off some steam." He pressed a button and dropped her from the call. "Why is she packing? For that matter, why are you still in the office this late at night?"

Jackson had a pregnant wife and a toddler. Gemma was a newlywed. Unlike Caleb, they had families to get home to.

"Urgent assignment straight from the police commissioner," Jackson said. "The whole team is flying out before dawn to investigate some human remains found in Algonquin Provincial Park. It could be a camping group that went missing over a decade ago. We'll be without cell phone or internet service most of the day, except when we get back to the main lodge at night. So, Gemma's printing off everything she can find about the case, while pulling every spare battery charger she can find. You'd think we were going off the grid for a month." He laughed. "Even Simcoe is up on the third floor with Hudson and me avoiding the chaos." Gemma's three-legged Australian shepherd and Jackson's much larger German shepherd had adopted each other like family.

"Wow." Caleb blew out a long breath. He didn't know what irked him more—the knowledge that his team was taking on a big case without him, or the fact he wouldn't be able to chat with them during the day. "I'm half tempted to cut my holiday short and come join you."

"I'm sure you are," Jackson said, "but you wouldn't make it back here before we leave. You've got to be in Toronto for Sheb's K-9 testing on Monday, and you know Finnick would tell you not to bail on your vacation."

"I know."

Since getting married at Christmas, Finnick had started reminding them all of the importance of building a well-rounded life outside of work. And not just in terms of their spouses and kids, but faith, community and hobbies too. In fact, he'd set an example by getting his helicopter pilot's license renewed and going flying on the weekends with Gemma's new husband, Patrick.

Except that some of us have been happy to only think about work, and aren't ready for that to change.

He burst through a door into the lobby, tightened his grip on Sheb's leash as he crossed through, then stepped out into the darkening parking lot. "Okay, I'm just leaving the hospital now."

Amethyst Harbour's hospital was smaller than the larger facilities in nearby Thunder Bay. It was set on the shores of Lake Superior, which provided beautiful views from the lounges when the sun was up.

"How are Hailey and Ferris?" Jackson asked. Caleb had filled Jackson and Gemma in with the play-by-play of the rescue and hospital visit—including the fact that Ferris was definitely his son. Not that he was ready to open that Pandora's box right now.

"All good," Caleb said. "Thankfully."

He turned away from the parking lot and onto a small path that led around the side of the building. He loosened his grip on Sheb's leash. Round pot lights embedded in the path shone like puddles beneath their feet. Planters sprung from either side. The dog sniffed his way toward them,

Caleb turned a corner and started down the dark and empty path that led along the waterfront.

"So, even though I'm still at the office, it's definitely after work hours," Jackson said. "What's going on with the case or cases?"

Case or cases, that was the question. Sheb whined and tugged at his leash, as if there was an animal or human friend lurking around the corner that he wanted to go say hello to. Caleb glanced back at the darkness. There was nobody there.

Caleb quickly ran Jackson through the details of everything that had happened, relieved to feel the familiar switches and wheels of his investigative-cop brain begin to click and turn.

"I honestly don't know if we're dealing with multiple cases here or one big complicated case," Caleb admitted. "The attacks on Hailey and Matty are pretty much identical. It would be impossible for any cop to look at both cases with an open mind and not immediately see it's a pattern. Especially considering the intended target could be Matty's twin sister, Phoebe."

"So, we don't think Hailey and Ferris were the intended targets?" Jackson said.

Ferris's bright inquisitive eyes and eager smile filled Caleb's mind. He pushed them away for now. He'd just managed to start thinking like a cop again. He wasn't ready to consider thinking like anything else.

Let alone a father....

"I don't know," Caleb admitted. "According to my dad, the police think Phoebe's the target, but my gut isn't sure. After all, Hailey had a run-in with the Goats just hours earlier, and the Goats did apparently incapacitate a security guard by slipping something into his soup once."

"Also, five years between the murders is a long gap," Jackson added.

"Agreed," Caleb said. "If there's a pattern here in terms of timing, I can't see it."

"Why would your cousin's killer start robbing banks and pawnshops in and around Thunder Bay?" Jackson asked.

"I don't know," Caleb said. "I'll admit it's a stretch. But alternatively, why would Hailey witness her colleague being murdered by the Goats and then get drugged on the same day?"

He tugged the leash lightly and Sheb heeled. Together, they walked down the waterfront path. The yellow glowing reflections of the lampposts shimmered on the black water of Lake Superior like fire.

"Well, your gut is right a lot," Jackson said. "At least half the time."

Caleb snorted.

"Phoebe is the sweetest person in the world," Caleb said. "I can't imagine anyone wanting to kill her."

"Could you imagine somebody wanting to kill Matty?" Jackson countered.

Caleb's footsteps slowed. He let the leash go as slack as he could without dropping it entirely, and Sheb wandered down to the waterfront and started exploring the rocks.

"Matty was really good-looking and charming," Caleb admitted. "All the girls in high school were attracted to him and that just carried on into adulthood."

Which might be why he'd never doubted that Hailey could've fallen for Matty too.

"We got a lot of attention from women at Renee's wedding," he went on, "Renee said almost all the bridesmaids had asked for his number."

"How many bridesmaids were there?" Jackson interjected.

"Eight," Caleb said. "All but Phoebe were from out of town. I always wondered if Matty broke someone's heart and she spiked his drink as revenge, not expecting it would kill him. The fact he was drugged with over-the-counter sleeping pills makes it look like a crime of opportunity. It might not have even been planned. My dad said they interviewed over three hundred people who were at the wedding or the diner the night he died."

"That's a pretty big suspect pool," Jackson said.

Sheb was still exploring the coastline and running up and down the water's edge. Caleb stopped walking and watched him.

"Accidental death, with jealousy as a motive," Jackson said. "Any other motives? What about money?"

"Hardly," Caleb said. "Phoebe and Matty's dad died when they were little. Their mom, Steff, struggled to get by. She was an office cleaner and then opened her own cleaning business when Phoebe and Matty were teenagers."

"Where is she now?"

"Dead," Caleb said, sadly. "My aunt was a beautiful person—kind, generous, understanding. She passed away in her sleep of a heart attack when Phoebe and Matty were about nineteen and away at summer camp."

"I'm sorry."

"Thanks. Phoebe owns the business now. Her fiancé, Daryl, is the manager."

"What's Daryl like?" Jackson asked.

"Business savvy," Caleb said, and shrugged. He watched as Sheb tried to nip and lick the small waves as they brushed his paws. Sheb was such an amazing dog. Caleb just didn't know if he was cut out for K-9 work. "He's alright. Teased me a lot growing up about who my dad was, but never in a vicious way. We never really clicked, but I've known him forever. He's the kind of guy who's always talking about raking in big bucks in his online investments, through precious metals, electronic currency, blockchain and other things that live in his phone. He's practically married to his phone."

Ironically, people could probably say the same about Caleb's relationship with work. He pushed the uncomfortable thought away.

"But you can't really judge a guy for succeeding at business," Caleb went on, "especially as he's incredibly generous with Phoebe and her kids."

Sheb stopped suddenly and sniffed the air, as if sensing some particularly interesting critter.

"Daryl sounds like the kind of person who criminals would target," Jackson said, "and he's getting married in three days? Maybe it's a copycat who went after Daryl's fiancée to extort or threaten him."

Suddenly, Sheb tensed. The dog's ears twitched and Caleb could sense a near-silent growl building in the dog's throat.

"Hang on," Caleb said, and his voice dropped to a whisper. "Sheb thinks we might not be alone."

He glanced up and down the waterfront. There was no one there.

"Are you sure?" Jackson asked.

"No," Caleb admitted. "But Sheb sure seems to be."

The dog was standing at full attention now. His snout rose and he sniffed the air. Caleb followed the direction and saw nothing but tall lampposts punctuated by long, dark shadows where the light didn't fall.

"I don't see anything—" Caleb started to say. Then the words froze on his tongue, as one of the shadows seemed to shift and move before his eyes, only to freeze again. Was he seeing things? He tightened his hand on Sheb's leash and started jogging back down the path, toward where he thought he'd seen the shadow move. "Actually, I'm not sure."

There was nothing there but a blank wall and grass. Not even a visible footprint on the ground to show somebody had been standing there.

"A moment ago, I thought I saw something move," Caleb said, "but there's no one there now. Just shadows. So, either Sheb's wrong or whoever's stalking me is really good at hide-and-seek."

"Gemma?" Jackon called. "Are the Goats known for being stealthy?"

"No." Gemma called back faintly. "But they are sure-footed. Why?"

"Sheb might be chasing shadows," Jackson said.

"Ask her what she knows about the security guard's soup," Caleb said.

The K-9's hackles rose. His growl grew louder. Caleb frowned. The last time Sheb had sensed danger, he'd been right.

He slipped the earpiece in his ear and switched his phone to it. Caleb could hear Gemma telling Jackson pretty much the same thing Chief Perry had about the soup.

"The Goats also tried carbon monoxide poisoning," Gemma went on, and Caleb could hear her crossing the floor toward her brother. "It's interesting, but not the kind of thing we can build a pattern around. Did you ask him what he's going to do about Hailey and Ferris?"

"No." Jackson sounded amused. "Remember how much you used to like me prying into your relationship with Patrick?"

"That was different."

"Because it was your private life that was being pried into?"

Caleb half tuned the siblings out and inched forward. Was that the faint sound of somebody moving just a few feet away around the corner of the building? Or was it just a breeze brushing the branches of a tree? Sheb's ears continued to twitch. His teeth seemed to be almost biting the air to get a better scent.

A hunch began to tingle at the back of Caleb's skull. Slowly, he reached into his pocket, pulled out the small cloth ball he used to run Sheb through his paces and slipped a treat inside it. Then he waved it beneath Sheb's nose. The K-9 pup turned toward it.

"I'm going to take Sheb for a run down the shoreline," Caleb said, loudly.

He switched the call to his earpiece again, opened the camera on his phone, then he tossed the ball as far as he could down the shore, in the opposite direction. Sheb woofed and ran after it, in a clattering of paws and jangling dog tags. Caleb raised the phone high and leaped around the corner.

"Corporal Caleb Perry!" he called and pressed the camera button. "Ontario Cold Case Task Force."

The camera flashed. The distraction had worked. For a fraction of an instant, Caleb saw a tall, bearded and hooded figure loom in front of him. Then a hand came out of nowhere, shoving him hard in the chest and sending him sprawling. Caleb lost his footing. The phone fell from his hand. Caleb grabbed it, leaped up and dashed after the man, just to see him disappearing down the side of the building.

"I've got eyes on the stalker!" Caleb shouted, as he signaled to Sheb. "Big guy, six-foot-four, black hoodie."

Jackson and Gemma shouted down the line, asking for details he didn't know and reminding Caleb to stay safe. The man disappeared into the parking lot. Caleb pressed himself faster. A motorcycle roared. Caleb reached the lot just in time to see the hooded figure roar out of the lot and disappear down the road into the darkness.

"I lost him." Caleb gasped a painful breath and quickly filled his colleagues in. "I think I got a picture though."

He checked his phone. Seemed all he'd managed to take a picture of were black and gray blurs. Caleb groaned and sat down on a nearby bench. Sheb trotted up, with his ball in his mouth, and laid his head on Caleb's leg. "Never mind, it's too blurry."

"Email it to me," Gemma said. "If there's anything there, I'll see if I can enhance it."

Caleb sent it to her. He heard the sound of a keyboard

clacking and a desk chair squeaking. He could tell by the echoes of the room that Jackson had put him on speaker-phone. A long, uncomfortable silence spread out as Gemma tinkered with the photo.

"So, while she's clearing up the picture," Jackson said, "do you want to talk to me about the kid?"

"Hailey looked me right in the eye and told me that Ferris is my son," Caleb said.

"Do you believe her?" Jackson asked.

"I do," Caleb admitted. "As stupid as it is to admit, I think I told myself that the fact Hailey had never called me back and pressed the issue meant she was lying and it wasn't true. But here, seeing Hailey face-to-face and meeting Ferris…"

His words trailed off.

"It's a lot to process," Jackson said.

"It is," Caleb said. "I don't even know how I feel right now. I was angry at first and now I'm kind of numb. I'll talk to her tomorrow and fill you in then."

"Well, whatever happens I'm here for you."

"I know. Thanks."

"Got it!" Gemma shouted. There was a loud bang that usually meant Gemma had hit her desk with both hands in triumph. "Sending it now."

He heard a swoosh, followed by a ping, and looked down to see a man's face appearing out of the picture of blurs he'd sent.

The man had a thick black beard. His eyes were half hidden in the hood of his sweatshirt.

"Now that's someone I wouldn't want to meet in a dark alley," Gemma said. "Recognize him?"

"No," Caleb admitted. "Never seen him before in my life."

"No hits on the system either," Gemma said. "But I'll see what I can find out."

Who are you? Caleb asked the face silently. *And why were you following me?*

Hailey sat on the edge of her hospital bed, wrapping up her interview with Chief Perry and two of the senior investigators she knew had also investigated everyone in connection with Matty's murder, including herself. She assumed that meant they were investigating whether the two cases were linked, but the police wouldn't confirm it for her one way of the other. Besides the worrying lack of answers, the police questioning had gone smoothly. Thankfully, they reassured her they'd ask the local police patrol to swing by Phoebe's house multiple times in the night in case somebody made a second attempt on Phoebe and her kids, and they'd send another patrol to keep an eye on Hailey's home.

After almost two hours of police questioning, punctuated by multiple medical check-ins by the doctor and nurses, the police left her alone with the doctor again, who gave her a clean bill of health, saying she'd successfully gotten the drugs out of her system and they were going to discharge her. The doctor added that she should get someone to stay with her overnight, in an overabundance of caution, just so that she wasn't alone if she suddenly felt woozy.

She was still getting herself turned around and wondering what to do next when a quiet knock came at the edge of the door, and she looked up to see Caleb's dad had returned on his own without the other investigators. Sylvester was a large man, with a generous white mustache and the quiet, level voice of a man who was able to project authority without getting loud or forceful. She knew it hadn't been easy for Caleb to grow up in his shadow. In fact, for as long as she could remember, everyone had just assumed Caleb would follow his father into local law enforcement, which had maybe been why Caleb had been so determined to move fifteen hours away.

"I just spoke with my wife," he said. "Alma asked me to pass on that we'd be very happy to have you and Ferris stay with us for as long as you need. We have a spare bedroom as well as Caleb's old room, so plenty of space for both of you."

"Thank you," she said, "I really appreciate it, but I'm just not sure what I want to do yet."

It was a very kind offer, but one that put her in an awkward position. Hailey was an only child. Her own parents lived on the other side of the country and were both struggling from health problems, which kept them from being actively involved in hers and Ferris's lives. While Sylvester and Alma had never directly come out and asked if they were Ferris's grandparents—let alone pushed Hailey for any kind of acknowledgement—they'd stepped up and been there for her and Ferris in every way she could've hoped for. From saving them seats in church whenever she and Ferris were running late, to stepping in to babysit whenever she was in a pinch, and dropping by with gifts on Ferris's birthday and Christmas. But as endlessly thankful as she was for them, she'd drawn a line at ever visiting their home or letting herself be fully enveloped in the family.

It just didn't seem right without talking to Caleb about it first—telling him that she'd been invited over to his parents' for this holiday or that and asking him how he felt about her going. Anything less would be too much like trying to sneak in the back door of something because she didn't have the courage to just walk up to the front door and knock.

It wasn't even that she expected him to tell her not to spend time in his family's home. It was that she'd wanted Caleb to be the one who invited her in.

Thankfully, she was rescued from having to answer by the resounding echo of about a dozen feet coming down the hallway toward her room. A moment later, Ferris rounded the corner with six-year-old River and Lake by his side. For a moment, the three kids jockeyed for position in the doorway, before Ferris ran over to hug Hailey, and the twins made a beeline to hug their "Great Uncle Sly." Then came Phoebe and Daryl. Hailey couldn't help but notice that Daryl had somehow managed to link Phoebe's fingers with one hand and check his cell phone with the other. It was like Daryl was addicted to his phone, or at least to the money he was able to make with it.

When the kids were done their hugs, Daryl slipped his phone in his pocket and greeted the police chief kindly, while Phoebe embraced Hailey. It was a warm and safe hug, and Hailey silently thanked God for her friend.

"Thanks for taking care of our girl Hailey," Daryl said to Sylvester, and shuddered. "The idea that some criminal miscreant is out to target my family just chills me to the bone. I can't wait until the wedding this weekend and for Phoebe and the kids to move in with me. Just let me know if there's anything I can do."

"You and Ferris are coming to stay at our home tonight," Phoebe told Hailey firmly. "Don't even try to argue. We've already set up the foldout couch for you in the living room and a sleeping bag in the twins' room for Ferris."

"Thank you," Hailey said.

That would mean local police just had one home to patrol.

"She even got me to set up the twins' old baby monitor,"

Daryl added, "so if Hailey so much as breathes funny in the night, Phoebe will know."

It took a few minutes to say their goodbyes to Sylvester and then for Hailey to finish checking out. Then the six of them piled into the brand-new SUV that Daryl had bought in preparation for his new role as a stepfather. Phoebe insisted on sitting in the back with the children and giving Hailey the passenger seat, which gave Hailey a bird's-eye view of the barrage of notifications that peppered Daryl's phone as he drove. Green arrows and numbers indicated some financial things were going up. Red arrows and more numbers indicated other money-related things were going down. Pink-and-purple boxes that seemed to be filled with abbreviations and symbols she couldn't decipher appeared to be urging Daryl to buy things. An orange box flashed across the screen announcing a typhoon would be hitting the coast on the other side of the world.

"Honey," Daryl called back to Phoebe, "can you please text Renee and tell her to tell Lenny to double our Whyy-art Inc. shares and be prepared to liquidate our QXT at ten percent? Also, get him to double-check the Pine Suds account for 260 Main and see if he can get them to extend our cleaning contract on the entire two-block radius for another six months?"

"On it!" Phoebe said and Hailey glanced back and watched as Phoebe sent the messages. Then she looked up and caught Hailey's gaze. "Daryl has landed Pine Suds huge contracts in Thunder Bay's industrial buildings. Plus, he's a genius when it comes to making money online. I can't claim to understand all the ins and outs of it—"

"Buy low," Daryl called out with a laugh, "sell high! And figure out what way the wind is blowing before everyone else does. It's as simple as that!"

Phoebe laughed too and rolled her eyes at him. "My husband-to-be is too humble," she said. The she leaned forward, away from the kids. "Truth is, when Mom died, Pine Suds was deep in the hole financially. Matty and I couldn't begin to figure out where the money had gone, and we'd barely managed to get our feet under us before Matty was gone too."

Sadness washed through her friend's eyes like a wave lapping the shore. But as Hailey watched, Phoebe blinked hard and her chin rose.

"But Daryl had always been there for me," she said, brightly. "Even when we were just friends, ever since the beginning."

"Her love and the kids are my greatest treasures," Daryl said. He reached back in between the seats for Phoebe's hand and squeezed it. A beautiful smile filled the bride-to-be's face, but Hailey could remember just how painful those times in Phoebe's life had been and all the tears she'd cried.

Despite all the chaos and fear that had rocked her day, it was that brief conversation in the SUV that Hailey found rolling around in her head later that night, as she lay curled up in animal-print sheets and superhero blankets on Phoebe's pullout couch.

Looking back, she was kind of embarrassed at how she'd behaved at Renee and Lenny's wedding. She'd just found out she was pregnant. She'd practically dove for Renee's bouquet, knowing that would put pressure on Caleb to propose. Then, when Caleb had broken her heart, they'd argued loudly, caused a scene and she'd left in floods of tears, only to be found by Matty later. Not her finest moment.

Ever since, there'd been this little ball of guilt that sat like a stone in a corner of her heart, telling her that if only she'd handled her breakup with Caleb better, Matty wouldn't have been with her at that diner, and then maybe Matty wouldn't have been drugged and killed. Even if he'd been drugged at the wedding, maybe he'd have been home safe in his bed before the sleeping pills had kicked in and he'd have been able to call 911 the moment he realized something was wrong. Or maybe he'd have still been at the wedding reception venue and surrounded by friends who'd have been able to rush him to the hospital.

Maybe Matty would've still been alive if it wasn't for her.

Not that she'd ever admitted that to anyone. Let alone Phoebe. Maybe because she'd known Phoebe would've told her she was being ridiculous and that Matty's death wasn't her fault, and Hailey wasn't ready to let go of that pain and regret just yet. Maybe, because she feared it was all that kept her from being the person she used to be.

He's my cousin and it would have been nice to have him at my wedding.

Phoebe's words from the other day floated in the back of her mind. *But Daryl thinks it would be a distraction. Plus, I wouldn't want to make things hard for you.*

The pain in her heart grew heavier. Hailey began to pray.

Lord, no matter what happens with Phoebe and Daryl's wedding, help me to turn all my messy and complicated feelings over to You.

The sound of footsteps creaking on the old wooden floors made her open her eyes and sit up.

"Did I wake you?" Phoebe was standing in the doorway with her cell phone in her hand.

Hailey shook her head. "No, I was just lying here, thinking and praying."

Phoebe sat down on the edge of the sofa bed. The springs creaked.

"I was just talking to Caleb," Phoebe said. "He wanted to

apologize to me for not being there for me when Matty died and also to reassure me that he didn't mean to make things awkward for me by coming to town. I think he should be at my wedding."

"I think so too." Hailey reached for her hand and gave it a quick squeeze. "And I promise if he does come, I won't cause any drama or be a distraction."

"I know," Phoebe reassured her, "and when I get back from my honeymoon, I promise that I'll be there for you and give you all the time you need to talk and process everything that's going on. Caleb also asked me to ask you if you're willing to meet up with him for coffee tomorrow morning. I'm happy to feed Ferris breakfast and take him to kindergarten for you." Her son was at the same school as her twins.

"Sounds like a plan." Hailey let out a long breath. Her boss had already given Hailey the day off work anyway. "I've got to go into Thunder Bay tomorrow morning to get a new phone. Thankfully, my phone was backed up online so they can just download all my data on to the new one. Can you text Caleb back and suggest we meet in the Grand Mall courtyard at eight forty-five?"

She'd also have to contact a mechanic when her car was eventually released from the police evidence lot and find out if it was salvageable. But she'd tackle one problem at a time. The mall was a neutral location, in a bigger city where they wouldn't have to worry about running into half of Amethyst Harbour while they talked. She could head to the phone store after.

Phoebe typed out a message to Caleb. There was a whoosh followed by a ding.

"Caleb says he'll see you there." Phoebe slid the phone back in her pocket. Then she straightened her engagement ring. "You know, I never imagined anyone would take care of me like Daryl has. He's actually chartered us a mini yacht for our honeymoon, although that's supposed to be a secret and he told me not to tell anyone. We're going to sail around Canadian and American waters by ourselves for the first week, then surprise the kids by picking them up and sailing all the way down to Florida together as a family."

Hailey reached for her hand and squeezed it. The ring dug into her skin. "I'm happy for you. Not just for the fancy stuff, but also the fact he seems really devoted to you."

Phoebe smiled. "Yeah, he is."

Truth was, Hailey had never understood what it was about Daryl that Phoebe had fallen for. He'd always seemed more interested in making money than connecting with people. While Phoebe, Steff and Matty had all been the type who'd give anyone who asked the shirt off their backs. Sometimes, she wondered if Phoebe had just been lonely and didn't want to raise her twins alone. And if so, it wasn't like Hailey could blame her. Plus, Daryl had always been driven—he'd worked longer hours than anyone she knew and had thrown that same relentless energy into being the perfect partner for Phoebe.

Maybe deep down Hailey was jealous. After all, she had fallen for a man who'd never once made her the center of his life. And even if Caleb was now willing to be a dad to Ferris, would Hailey ever be able to really trust him back in her heart?

Phoebe returned to her bed and Hailey went back to trying to sleep. Although, she must've managed to doze off at some point, because the next thing she knew, dazzling sunshine was streaming through the windows and all three children were bounding onto the sofa bed while Phoebe called them all to come for breakfast.

Hailey had been planning to rely on taxis or maybe rent a car, but instead Daryl swung by before going to work at Pine Suds to give Phoebe a ride to work and the children a ride to school, giving Hailey the opportunity to use Phoebe's older car for the time being. Phoebe also offered to take Ferris with them to the pool after school, to play in the water while the twins had swimming lessons. She'd swing by Hailey's home later to grab his bathing suit.

Daryl then added it was warm enough for him to drive his two-seater convertible and let Phoebe have the SUV until Hailey had her car back. So, after a flurry of hugs and an extra-long hug while saying a second goodbye to Ferris, she left for the mall.

The sun continued to shine bright as Hailey made her way west along the shoreline to the city of Thunder Bay, blinding her eyes whenever she glanced back in the rearview mirror, even after donning the pair of sunglasses she'd found in Phoebe's glove compartment.

Despite all the deep breaths she'd taken and prayers she'd silently spoken, her heart was still full of dancing butterflies as she pulled slowly into the mostly empty parking lot.

A white van pulled off the road and followed her into the lot. The same van had actually been behind her on the road for a while, but it had been following at a normal distance she hadn't thought anything of it. After all, there was only one main road from Amythest Harbour to Thunder Bay, and a lot of people had reasons to be at the mall. Her shoulders tensed for a moment, then relaxed again as the van stopped and parked several rows away from her.

Instead, her eyes were drawn to the tall, handsome man with the incredible smile who was currently jogging around the perimeter of the parking lot with a joyfully unwieldy Belgian Malinois by his side. She parked, got out and just stood there for a long moment, watching Caleb and Sheb run. The butterflies in her heart flapped faster until it almost felt like they were punching her in the gut.

After all this time, Caleb was still the most handsome man she'd ever seen in her life.

No matter how many incredible men she'd met through friends or church over the past few years, none had sparked so much as the tiniest flutter in her heart. And now that she was almost face-to-face with Caleb again, she was frustratingly even more attracted to him than ever. And it wasn't just his outward appearance. That kind of thing was temporary and the kind the thing she'd learned to see through. What attracted her to him now was deeper than that. It was the way he'd stayed with Ferris in her hospital room and kept her son happy, distracted and occupied. It was the patience he had with Sheb. And how he'd seemed to come alive when he talked about his team.

She wasn't sure if it was Caleb or Sheb who noticed her first, but they both stopped running in tandem and looked her way. Suddenly, Sheb barked out a warning and concern flashed across Caleb's face. They ran toward her.

"What's wrong?" she called.

"Behind you!" Caleb shouted.

Too late, she heard the footsteps pounding toward on the cement. Then even before she could turn, a hand clamped hard on her shoulder, jostling her forward.

SEVEN

For Caleb, everything seemed to happen in an instant. A thin young man with shaggy hair had run up to Hailey, grabbed her and nearly knocked her over. Sheb barked and Caleb shouted at the man to let Hailey go.

But instead of falling, Hailey spun toward the man as her elbow rose in self-defense. She clocked the man squarely in the nose. The young man swore and fell to the ground, clutching his face and screaming that Hailey had broken his nose.

Caleb and Sheb reached Hailey's side. They flanked Hailey protectively and Caleb yanked out his badge. Sheb then positioned himself between Hailey and the man still shouting on the ground.

"It's okay," Hailey, brushing her hand over Caleb's arm. "It's just Gordo, my colleague."

Caleb looped a finger around his K-9's collar and ordered Sheb to stand down. Hailey reached past them for Gordo's hand.

"I'm sorry!" she said. "You startled me."

"What was that for?" Gordo ignored her hand and climbed to his feet.

"You grabbed me and nearly knocked me over—"

"I only wanted to talk to you!" Gordo protested. "After all, our friend Jet was killed yesterday!"

Caleb crossed his arms over his chest. He doubted Hailey needed the reminder. Jet had been killed in front of her. Gordo's voice was both whiny and manipulative. Not to mention, Caleb could tell his nose wasn't actually broken, although he might have a decent bruise from the wallop. But Gordo's eyes were glassy and his pupils were the size of saucers. The young man was definitely high.

"What are you doing here?" Hailey asked.

"I followed you from Amethyst Harbour," Gordo said. "I'm in trouble and need some money to get out of town."

"What kind of trouble?" Hailey asked.

Gordo's eyes darted to Caleb, like he was debating asking the other man to back off so Gordo could speak to Hailey without him. Not that Caleb was about to leave Hailey alone, unless he was sure she was okay.

"I need money," Gordo said. "I need to leave town. I think the Goats are going to kill me because they know about Pepper—"

"Who's Pepper?" Hailey interjected.

"Hot Pepper," Gordo said. "My online girlfriend. She asked me all these questions about my work, I told her all about the bank and I promised her that I'd be there yesterday instead of you when the Goats showed up and killed Jet. But then I called in sick."

Hailey and Caleb exchanged a glance.

"You met a woman online?" Caleb asked.

"And told her all about the bank?" Hailey asked.

"Do you know what she looks like?" Caleb added. "Or her real name?"

"No, but I've seen pictures." Gordo was rambling now.

He swayed from one foot to another. "It's not her fault the Goats showed up and killed Jet—"

"Are you sure?" Hailey cut him off. "Gordo, if there's even the slightest chance you were actually feeding information to the Goats themselves—"

Gordo swore so loudly her words were swallowed up in the sound. Hailey winced as a string of ugly words flew from Gordo's mouth, calling her every eye-wateringly ugly name in the book.

"Hey!" Caleb stepped forward. "That's enough."

Gordo stopped his onslaught on Hailey and turned to Caleb. "Aren't you the scumbag who left Hailey to raise her kid all by herself?"

Hailey bristled. Caleb's jaw clenched.

"Sure am," Caleb said and his chin rose. "I'm Corporal Caleb Perry, member of the Cold Case Task Force. You don't seem like you should be driving right now. Can we call you a cab?"

Gordo stammered a string of barely intelligible syllables, including the fact he was a good guy, hadn't grabbed Hailey "that hard" and that what happened to Jet wasn't his fault. Then he stormed off toward a greasy diner that lay at one end of the mall.

Caleb looked back at Hailey, who was already on the phone with the police, reporting what Gordo had said and where to find him.

"The police will pick him up," she said after she ended the call. "They'll detox him and then question him about this Hot Pepper character. He's in no state to answer any questions until he gets sober."

"Do you think he fed the Goats information?" Caleb asked.

"I wouldn't be surprised," Hailey said.

Caleb loosened is grip on Sheb and the three of them started walking the opposite direction toward the entrance at the far end of the mall.

"I'm sorry about that," Hailey added.

"Not your fault," Caleb said. He slipped his phone back in his pocket, mentally adding Gordo to the growing list of things he was planning on talking to the team about. "He's clearly going through something. Hopefully, when police pick him up it'll lead to some solid information."

"I have no idea," Hailey said. "But he had no right to call you a scumbag like that."

"He called you far worse," Caleb said, and shrugged. "Plus, I figured he was just saying what everybody else is already thinking about me."

"Hey." Hailey stopped walking reached out and grabbed his hand. To his surprise, he let her take it. "I have no idea what other people said. But I never said that about you. I never bad-mouthed you or let people bad-mouth you around me. I won't pretend I didn't cry buckets on Phoebe's shoulder, but I never tried to hurt you."

"I never meant to hurt you either," Caleb admitted. He felt his voice drop. His fingers slid in between hers, and for a long moment neither of them pulled away.

Then Hailey stepped back. "You accused me of cheating with you on your cousin, and I still don't know why."

Her tone had been flat—even matter-of-fact—but that didn't stop her words from stinging. She turned and started walking toward the building again. He and Sheb matched her pace.

"I'm sorry I hurt you," Caleb said. The automatic doors didn't open for them, probably because it wasn't yet nine. "But I honestly believed that Matty would never lie to me about something like that."

He grabbed for the oversized handle of the regular glass door that stood beside the sliding one, pulled it open and held it for Hailey and Sheb to walk through. But instead, Hailey stopped walking.

Her face had suddenly gone as pale as if the air had just been knocked out of her.

"Wait what?" she asked. "Matty told you that he and I were involved? Why would Matty ever lie about me like that?"

"I don't know," Caleb said. Neither of them moved. The door seemed to grow heavier in his hand. "But he was the one who told me you were pregnant, and that Ferris was his."

Hailey opened her mouth but no words came out.

"That's…really, really hard for me to believe," she managed finally.

Hailey turned and walked into the mall, as if trying to put distance between herself and what Caleb had just said. Caleb and Sheb followed. For a long moment, the three of them just walked through the long hallways, which were empty except for a handful of senior citizens in a mall-walkers club and a smattering of people on their way in to work.

Finally, they reached the courtyard. Tall windows arched above them, giving way to skylights. Towering ferns sprouted from marble planters. Metal garage-style doors covered the fronts of the shuttered stores. Somehow, without saying a word, it was decided that Hailey would go grab a table and Caleb would head to the open coffee kiosk. Hailey chose a quiet table for two, surrounded by ferns near a high-end jewelry store.

It wasn't until he was back with two iced coffees and a cup of ice cubes for Sheb that he'd forgotten to ask if she still took her iced coffee with almond milk and maple syrup. But the very faint smile that crossed her lips when she took a sip told him that she did.

"My immediate instinct was to call you a liar," Hailey admitted softly, drawing his attention back to her face. "In fact, I've been fighting the urge ever since you said it and it took me this long to calm down. Because I don't want to believe that Matty would've ever said anything like that about me."

She set her hands on the table with her palms slightly open. Her fingers were just inches away from his and he found himself wanting to reach for them.

"I get it," Caleb said. "I never believed Matty would lie to me about something like that either. From my perspective, I lost sight of both you and Matty at Renee and Lenny's wedding, so I had no idea you'd left together. Later, when I found out he was killed, I discovered he'd been seen in a diner later that night, holding hands with a woman on what looked like a date—"

Hailey's mouth shot open again, like she was about to contradict him. But instead, she tightened her fingers into fists, closed her mouth and nodded to Caleb to keep going.

"I assumed that this mystery woman was the one who'd killed him," Caleb said. "When I found out it was you, I felt like you'd lied by omission by not telling me you'd left the wedding with Matty the night he died. I figured you had to know something and was furious that you weren't doing more to help the investigation. I was devastated."

"Me too."

Slowly, the metal shop front doors began to rise up and down the hallways, roaring like intermittent thunder. Piped-in music switched on, filling the air with the soft sound of jazz.

Caleb put his phone on the table and opened the voice memos.

"Matty recorded a voice memo for me before he died and tried to send it to me," he said. "It was literally in his email outbox. But it was large file and he was in an area where the cell signal was low, so I didn't actually get it until days later when a CSI tech plugged it in at the lab to download its contents."

He hit Play.

"Hey, C-Man!" Matty's voice suddenly filled the air. Immediately, his cousin's face filled his mind, with his too-wide smile and unruly mop of dark curls. Suddenly, he felt Hailey reach for his hands and grab them. He grabbed them back and held on tight. "Just want you to hear it from me. Hailey's having my kid. I've been in love with her since kindergarten and I'm going to marry her. So, don't worry about anything, C-Man. Just head off to the great big city and go be a supercop. I know you can do it. This is Matty, by the way. Bye."

For a long moment, Caleb stared down at the phone on the table and their linked hands.

"It says a lot about my father's integrity as a police chief that the contents of this voice memo were never leaked and turned into town gossip," he said. "I've listened to it so many times I've memorized it. I've always suspected he had feelings for you. Maybe I was a bit insecure about it too, because I thought he was a better man than me. I mean, every girl in high school had a crush on him—"

"Not me," Hailey said, softly.

He swallowed hard. "I still don't understand why he'd have claimed you guys had a relationship behind my back if it wasn't true."

Then he looked up at her face. Tears shone in Hailey's

eyes. Then one began to roll down her cheek. Immediately, he pulled his hand free from hers, reached across the small table and brushed the tear away. He cupped her cheek with his hand.

"Hey." His voice grew husky in his throat. "It's okay."

They'd both lost someone they'd cared for deeply. And oh, how Caleb now wished he'd been there for Hailey and let her be there for him.

"He told me that he'd always loved me," Hailey said, and her voice dropped until it was barely above a whisper. Her blue-green eyes looked deeply into his. "He asked me to marry him. He said we'd raise the kid together and be a family. I didn't say yes—I didn't love him in a romantic way." She sighed. "Now, having been drugged with even a small dose of what hit him," she went on, "all I can think is that his feelings for me were real, but his actions had everything to do with the drugs in his system."

"I think in his own addled way, Matty was trying to be a hero and save us both from dealing with a difficult situation," Caleb said and looked down at their linked hands. "He was trying to rescue us."

He was trying to rescue me from having to face the mess I'd made, and the fact I'd treated this incredible woman as far less loved, important and valued than she deserved.

More garage-type doors rattled open around them. Voices rose and people began to fill the mall as the stores opened for the day. Sheb woofed softly and began to sniff at the air.

But still Caleb didn't pull away, neither did Hailey. Instead they just sat there, leaning across the small round table, with their faces just inches away from each other.

"Matty knew your dream was moving to Toronto and joining the RCMP K-9 unit," Hailey said. "He didn't want you to feel you had to quit your dream job, stay in Amethyst Harbour—"

"But I would have," Caleb protested. "If you'd called me right back, told me to stop being foolish and insisted Ferris was mine, I'd have eventually listened and stepped up—"

"And what?" Hailey cut him off in turn. "Married me out of duty? Why would I spend the rest of my life married to a man who didn't *want* to be married to me?"

He let her go and sat back as suddenly as if her words had physically punched him in the gut. That wasn't fair, was it? And yet, he hadn't been ready to step up and be her husband back then. He hadn't been willing to give Hailey his heart. So how dare he let himself accept the love she'd freely offered him? What right did a jaded man have to be loved by a woman like Hailey? None. Not until he was ready to fully give his life to her in return.

Before he could find his breath, Sheb barked. It was a quick, sharp bark that told Caleb to pay attention.

"Sheb thinks something's wrong," Caleb started, but before he could figure out what, the K-9 howled. Immediately, Caleb leaped to his feet and so did Hailey. Then he turned to the dog and signaled with his fingers. "Show me."

Sheb sat and whimpered softly.

"His instincts have been one hundred percent right so far," Caleb said. "It's his tracking that keeps failing. He can't figure out how to lead me to whatever he's sensing."

"Which means it's up to us to find what he's worked up about," Hailey said.

Yeah. Silently, Hailey and Caleb stood side by side and scanned the mall.

Lord, help me see what we need to see.

At first, Caleb couldn't spot anything out of the ordinary. Customers lined up for coffee and doughnuts in the food court. Others trickled into stores.

As Caleb slowly turned and scanned the mall 360 degrees, he caught the dark blot of a single dull gray door, still closed, which stood out like an ugly shadow in the middle of the bright color of activity and light surrounding them. Hailey saw it too and grabbed his arm.

"The jewelry store is still closed," she whispered. "It's the only one not open."

She pulled away from him and moved toward the jewelry store. He looped his fingers through Sheb's collar to quiet the dog and followed half a step behind. Now he could see that somebody had in fact tried to open the rolling garage door from the inside, only to leave it a few inches open.

Sheb growled softly in a warning so deep Caleb could feel it in his own spine.

Hailey stopped a couple of feet away from the jewelry store, crouched down and looked under the gap—and her face paled. Immediately, Caleb dropped to the floor in push-up position, following her gaze.

He saw Gruff ransacking the jewelry cases, while Billy stood over a terrified young salesclerk, pressing the tip of his gun into the back of her head.

Hailey's heart beat so hard in her chest that for moment she was afraid the Goats would be able to hear it. Billy's finger shook on the trigger. The memory of Jet lying dead on the pavement filled her mind in a painful flash of red.

One wrong move—any wrong move—and Billy would pull the trigger either on purpose or by accident, and the young clerk would be dead.

The gap under the partially open rolling door was barely six inches. Time froze as Hailey glanced in fearful silence from the clerk's tearstained face to where Caleb was hunched down beside her. His palms were braced against the ground, with Sheb's leash still looped around one hand. The pup whined softly and tugged on the leash.

"I'll call dispatch," he whispered, "and coordinate rescue. You alert security and clear the mall. We've just got to be really careful and not put any of the civilians in here in danger."

"Or put the hostage in any more danger than she's already in," Hailey whispered back as quietly as she could. "Platinum does this store's armed vehicle transfers. The place has a back door and a small loading bay. The Goats must've snuck in the back, jumped the clerk when she was opening up, and presumably they plan to slip out the same way without getting caught."

Caleb nodded. "Got it."

Hailey kept her eyes locked on the terrified hostage. The clerk was barely twenty and pleading for her life through sobs with huge, scared eyes. Her name tag read Delia.

One wrong move and Delia could die.

Please Lord, help us save her life. I can't just let Billy kill someone else.

Not while I have the hope of saving them.

Caleb crouched, pulled out his phone and dialed. Sheb wriggled out of his grasp. Before either of them could stop him, the Belgian Malinois puppy crawled through the gap and disappeared into the store.

"Sheb!" Caleb gasped. "No!"

But it was too late. The dog was already running through the store, barking and snarling at the Goats. As they watched in horror, Billy raised his gun, pointed it at Sheb and fired. Sheb howled defiantly and swerved, as if the heroic dog had suddenly decided to launch his own solo rescue mission. The bullet burst through a display of engagement rings, narrowly missing the K-9.

"God, please keep my foolish dog safe," Caleb prayed. "I don't know what's gotten into him."

Neither did Hailey. But Sheb was providing a very effective distraction. Delia lay there shaking on the floor. And Hailey saw a chance to save her.

"Get help!" she told Caleb. "I'm going in!"

"Don't!" he started.

But she'd already started sliding under the gap and into the store, careful not to push the door open any further, knowing the ruckus of the rolling metal would certainly draw the Goats attention. She prayed silently that God would help her get the hostage out and get home to Ferris safely. Yes, she was putting her own life on the line, but what kind of mother would she be to Ferris if she let a woman die in front of her, when she had the chance to save her? Delia was lying terrified on the floor, with her hands clasped over her head. Sheb was running erratic laps around the store, picking up speed as he darted between the shelves and displays, and snapping at Billy and Gruff as he sped past. No one seemed to even notice Hailey as she slithered on her stomach through the narrow gap.

Okay, all she had to do was hide behind the counter, signal Delia to crawl toward her, and then they'd escape together along with Sheb as Caleb mobilized police to surround the store and take down the Goats.

Then suddenly, the hem of Hailey's shirt caught on the metal edge of the sliding door. For a terrifying second, she was stuck there, her body half in and half out of the store, with no way to move forward or back. She felt Caleb yank the fabric free. Then, instead of pulling her back out as she suspected he wanted to, his strong hands grabbed a hold of her feet and pushed her forward through the gap. She crawled through into the store and hid behind the counter from the amateurish chaos erupting around her. She looked back to see Caleb on the phone with police. Surely, dozens of other people in the mall must've heard the commotion by now and be calling the cops too.

She prayed the police would get there in time. He flashed her a thumbs-up, confidence filling his gaze, and she felt a fresh strength fill her core.

Then she turned back, crouched and peeked around the edge of the counter. Sheb was still barking and running wildly as Billy tried and failed to shoot anywhere near him. Gruff was scrambling to grab whatever he could and stuffing jewelry haphazardly into a bag.

"Delia!" Hailey whispered, calling to the cowering clerk. "Delia!"

Delia looked up.

Hailey gestured to her, coaxing her toward her. "Come on! This way!"

A glass case to her right shattered. Delia's whole body was shaking so hard her limbs seemed to quiver. Empathy filled Hailey's heart. She could call to Delia all she wanted, but it would do no good if fear gripped the young woman's body so tightly that Delia wasn't able to move.

Delia whimpered and shook her head. "I can't. They'll shoot me." Sirens blared on the other side of the door now. The mall was being evacuated as Caleb got people to safety.

"Come on!" Gruff shouted at Billy. "Stop wasting bullets! Ignore the dog, kill the witness and let's go!"

It was now or never. Hailey took a deep breath and crawled out from behind the relative protection of the counter, then grabbed ahold of Delia's hand. It trembled like a twig in a windstorm.

"Trust me," Hailey said. "I'll get you out of here."

Delia nodded. Hailey turned and crawled back toward the door half pulling, half guiding Delia along with her. For a moment the patterned tile seemed to stretch out indefinitely in front of her as the sound of swearing, shouting, barking, bullets firing and glass shattering seemed to swirl around her.

"This way!" Caleb whispered urgently through the crack in the door. "Come on! I've got you!"

Then she saw Caleb reaching for her and Delia through the gap. Sheb finally turned and crawled back out of the store to the safety of the other side.

Rescue was coming. Caleb was just inches away. It was going to be okay.

Then a single bullet sounded so close to Haley's head that her ears began to ring. She heard Delia cry out in pain, felt her hand go limp in hers and knew that Delia had been shot.

"Hailey Blue!" She heard Billy yell in his deep distorted voice. She looked back up to see Billy striding toward her, with his red-eyed goat mask, thick-soled cowboy boots and a long gray denim trench coat like some kind of terrifying cartoon villain. "I'm sick and tired of you! It's time I put an end to you once and for all!"

EIGHT

Billy strode across the floor toward Hailey and raised the gun toward her head, but he never got a chance to fire, as suddenly the door flew up with a deafening rattle and Caleb lunged through, with Sheb by his side and together they threw themselves at the Goat.

Billy fired. But the bullet flew wild as Sheb's strong jaws clamped down on Billy's ankle and Caleb grabbed Billy's hands and forced them above his head. Gruff turned and dashed out the back door. Billy shouted in pain and tried to kick his foot free, as the two men wrestled for the gun. Hailey turned to Delia. The young woman's face was pale, her eyes were closed and blood seeped from her side. Hailey yanked off her sweatshirt and pressed it over the woman's wound to stop the bleeding. She needed to get her to safety but didn't want to risk moving her either.

She heard Caleb grunt, Sheb snarl and the deafening sound of metal crashing against metal, an engine roaring, more bullets flying but this time from somewhere farther away, and then the sound of tires squealing. Still, she kept her focus on the woman now bleeding out on the floor in front of her, afraid of what would happen if she let go of Delia before medical help arrived.

Lord, please save her life. Don't let this woman die.

An eerie and unnatural stillness seemed to fall around her, as if the increasing sounds of sirens and voices she could now hear rising from beyond the walls were somehow being muffled and faded. Nothing mattered except keeping Delia alive.

Finally, she felt Caleb kneel down beside her and Sheb nudge her side with his warm snout.

"It's okay," Caleb said, softly. "It's all over. You can let her go now. Paramedics are here."

She blinked and looked up, and it was like all the noise and action around them suddenly rushed back into her field of vision again. Medics in bright yellow uniforms were running toward her. Police poured in from seemingly all directions. Caleb gently took her arm, helped Hailey to stand up and step back as emergency crews rushed in and took over caring for Delia. It was only then that she looked through the open door to the store's back room and noticed the gaping hole in the outside wall where the back exit had been. "What happened?"

"Gruff rammed his van through the outside wall and broke down the door," Caleb said. "Billy took advantage of it to slip out of my grip for a second, and before I could tackle him again, Gruff opened fire to give Billy enough cover to escape." He ran his hand over the back of his head. "Honestly, my top priority was keeping you guys safe, not chasing after them. I can only hope the cops get them. I mean, the front of the van is completely smashed. They're bound to find them."

"I'm so sorry," Hailey said. "I was so focused on keeping Delia alive it was like everything else in the world was suddenly on mute."

"Yeah," Caleb said, "I know how that is. When fight-or-flight mode just takes over and all that matters is survival, or in this case somebody else's survival."

She nodded and followed Caleb and Sheb away from of the wreckage of the jewelry store and through the maze of yellow police tape that was still in the process of being wrapped around the scene. By the look of things, the entire mall had been emptied out and shut down. Delia was taken to hospital and Hailey was checked out by paramedics, then questioned by police and this time, unlike after the bank heist, Caleb and Sheb stayed close by, never straying farther from her side than absolutely necessary.

But to her frustration, the mental fog that had fallen over her while trying to save Delia's life still hadn't cleared completely by the time they were done. As she and Caleb walked out of the mall and back to their vehicles, she suspected Caleb had noted it too, as the three of them passed his vehicle and walked toward the one she'd borrowed from Phoebe.

"Are you good to drive?" Caleb asked. "Or would you like me to give you a ride?"

She ran both hands through her hair. "Thanks, but I'm good."

"Glad to hear it." Caleb scanned his phone, flipped through some messages and frowned. Then he turned to Hailey.

"Can I be really honest with you a second?" he asked. The blue of his eyes seemed brighter and less guarded than she'd seen in years. "No agenda, no hidden motive, just straight up?"

She nodded. "Yes."

He glanced at his phone one more time, sighed deeply, then slid it into his pocket.

"I feel alone right now," Caleb admitted, "in a way I haven't felt since Matty died."

"Oh." She didn't know what she'd expected to hear, but it wasn't that.

"We just went through all that with the Goats, and all I want is to just talk it out with someone," Caleb said. "But technically I'm on still on holiday and my team is all in Algonquin Provincial Park right now, working on a case somewhere with no cell phone service, which means I've gone from casually chatting with my colleagues all day every day to sudden radio silence."

"I'm sorry," Hailey said. "That must be really hard."

She took a step toward him on the pavement. Her arms flinched instinctively, as if wanting to reach out and hug Caleb. Then she realized that despite doing her best to clean herself off with wipes the paramedics had given her, she still had traces of Delia's dried blood on her hands.

"Yeah," Caleb said. "They're like a family to me and not having them to talk to feels like losing a limb. Plus, I haven't had breakfast and I'm guessing neither did you. Hailey, you used to one of my best friends. You knew me better than anyone. Would you be okay if we just agreed to put the swords down, go grab food and talk about what all just happened?"

"Yeah," Hailey said, automatically, without hesitating long enough to argue with herself this time. Maybe it was because she was still in a daze. Or maybe she'd was starving and, truth was, she wanted to talk with someone too. Normally, she'd have called Phoebe, but her best friend was already rearranging her day to take care of Ferris and had more than enough on her plate with her wedding rehearsal tomorrow night, and the wedding was the morning after.

"Why don't we head back to my house? It's quiet and I've got plenty of coffee."

"Deal." Caleb grinned. It was an almost shy grin—the kind she hadn't seen on his face for years. "I'll grab doughnuts and meet you there."

She drove home, stopping at an alternative phone store on the way to see if they'd be able to give her a temporary cell to tide her over until the mall reopened. By the time Hailey had gotten home, washed and changed into a soft white T-shirt and sweatpants, Caleb was already walking up to her front door with Sheb by his side and a huge red box of doughnuts in his hands.

She felt a smile cross her face as she let them into her home and led the way into the kitchen, scooping up stray stuffed animals and little cars as she went, and dumping them in Ferris's toy box. Brightly colored children's drawings covered every available inch of kitchen wall space. She started the drip coffee maker as Caleb set the doughnuts on the table, and Sheb lay out in the long narrow sunbeam that stretched across the floor. Light small talk about her home, Ferris and the weather bounced back and forth between them, like a fragile balloon that both of them were trying hard not to pop.

The coffee finished percolating, and Hailey brought two mugs, two spoons, milk, sugar and the coffee pot over to the table. They each poured themselves a cup, sat down at the small table across from each other and lapsed into silence again, which neither of them seemed ready to break. She suspected they both needed a minute to catch their breath after this morning. Hailey let the mug warm her hands. It was actually nice to have a moment of peace.

"I'm sorry again for everything that happened after

Matty died." Caleb broke the quiet first. "I wish I could go back and do that phone call with you all over again."

"I'm sorry too," Hailey admitted. "I know I should've called you back and tried to talk to you about Ferris, but I was so overwhelmed and angry...and hurt."

She'd forgotten just how much of a fog she'd been in back then. The only thing that had mattered was protecting Ferris—this tiny little unexpected child she hadn't even met yet.

"It was like I was drowning in grief," she said, "and it took all the energy I had just to stay afloat. I had to quit a job that I loved, because I just couldn't look at a badge or a uniform without thinking about you and Matty. I cried all the time. And when the pain did start to clear, I just took all the energy I had and focused it on being the best possible mom to Ferris."

"You're a great mom and he's a fantastic kid," Caleb said, "You loved him and took care of him. That's what matters."

She'd thought so at the time, but it was nice to hear him say it too. She took another sip of coffee. Her hands still smelled like soap. She'd scrubbed them raw when she'd got home.

"Do you think Delia's going to make it?" she asked.

"Last I heard, they were going to rush her straight into surgery," Caleb said. "She lost a lot of blood, but hopefully the bullet didn't hit anything vital. They've also confirmed that police have taken Gordo into custody and are questioning him about Hot Pepper."

"I'm glad for that." But it didn't stop her from feeling guilty that she hadn't managed to get Delia out sooner. She set her mug down. "Do you think it's my fault that Delia got shot?"

"No!" Caleb was so emphatic the word almost exploded across the table at her. "You and Sheb might've saved her life."

"Might've," she repeated. "But we'll never know for sure what would've happened if I'd gotten her out sooner. Or if I could've done something different to prevent her from being shot. Just like we'll never know if Matty would still be alive if he and I hadn't hung out that night."

"Or," Caleb said, "maybe if you hadn't been with Matty that night, he might've passed out in traffic and taken a bunch of other people's lives with him. We don't know. We will never know." He took a deep breath and let it out slowly. "Hindsight isn't actually twenty-twenty. Even though it's really easy to look back at the past and fool yourself into thinking it is."

"It was certainly easier to blame myself," Hailey said, "than admit horrible things happen and I can't stop them."

Caleb chuckled sadly. "That's the truth."

Tears filled her eyes and she wasn't even sure why. Wordlessly, Caleb stood, opened his arms. She stood up and stepped into them. He hugged her and she hugged him back.

It was a warm hug and a kind one—the type that didn't need words or explanations. It was like for years she'd been rebuilding her life after being shipwrecked in a storm, and suddenly happened upon a fellow survivor who'd been recovering from being struck by the exact same storm. She still no idea how they were going to build anything together going forward. How was she going to share custody of Ferris with Caleb when he lived so far away? And what would happen if she let herself open her heart back up to the very man who'd broken it? She couldn't let herself be vulnerable, let alone risk getting hurt. Yes, they'd cleared the air and yes, Caleb seemed to have changed since he left, but that didn't mean she was ready to welcome him back into her life as anything more than Ferris's long-distance dad.

But for now, she could at least decide to stop waging war in her heart against Caleb. She could forgive him. She could accept his forgiveness too. And while there might be a whole bunch of battles she didn't know how they were going to win, they could at least call a truce and agree to stop fighting this one.

Slowly, she pulled away from the hug. Caleb pulled away too, and they sat down, went back to their coffees and doughnuts, and began talking again.

"Let's start with just the facts on this case for now," Caleb said, "before moving on to any theories. No right or wrong answers, just everything that we can remember. Do you have something we can make notes on?"

"I'm sure I can find something." She went and rummaged around in the drawer of a small desk that sat under the window. It was covered in plants in brightly painted flowerpots she'd made with Ferris. What once had been a craft drawer was now a miscellaneous hodgepodge of clay, pipe cleaners, abandoned cables, uncapped markers and other various things she didn't know where to put anywhere else.

"Okay I've got a pencil and a mostly empty spiral notebook," she called. "I've got some actual pens somewhere, if I can figure out where Ferris's craft box has gone. Sorry, my house is better set up for four-year-olds than policework."

She laughed and Caleb chuckled as he glanced around at the colorful mosaic of artwork surrounding the walls.

"The pencil's fine," he said, and she dropped her spoils of her hunt down on the table. "And I'm looking forward to hearing Ferris tell me more about all his pictures. I'm sure he has fantastic stories for all of them."

She smiled and sat. "He does."

"Okay." Caleb turned to the notepad. "Step one is we try to get all the facts that we can think of down on paper, as fast as we can before either of us forget anything important. Then steps two and three will be trying to find patterns and strategize next steps."

Together, they talked through absolutely everything they remembered about the Goats and their crime spree. After that, they jotted down everything both of them could remember about how Hailey had been drugged with the grapefruit drink the day before. Then finally, they moved on to what they both remembered about the suspiciously similar thing that had happened to Matty five years earlier.

It was the first time Hailey had actually talked through what had happened with Matty from a purely fact-based perspective without letting her emotions overwhelm her. She suspected it was true for Caleb too. Then they talked through the awkward encounter with her colleague Gordo in the parking lot.

"Sorry," Caleb said and smacked his forehead. "It completely slipped my mind earlier, but I saw a large man following me outside the hospital last night."

He pulled out his phone, and she looked down at the tall and imposing bearded man.

"I've never seen him before," she said.

"Me neither."

They kept talking and Caleb wrote quickly, filling page after page. It reminded her of the kind of conversations she and Caleb would have when working a case, back when they were both local police officers and colleagues. Not that anything they were jotting down now seemed to be any different than anything she'd told the police during any of the multiple times she'd been questioned. Or that either of them had any major flashes of insight or revelation. Still, it was a good exercise. It was freeing.

A knock sounded at the front door, followed by the doorbell chiming. Sheb leaped to his feet and woofed. Hailey glanced out the front window to see an SUV in the driveway. Daryl was sitting in the driver's seat and Phoebe was standing at the door. Judging by the empty back seats, they'd dropped by before picking up the kids from school. It was only then she glanced at the clock and realized that she and Caleb had been talking for hours.

"I forgot she's taking Ferris swimming after school." She leaped up. "Give me a second. I've got to grab his swim bag."

"No problem," Caleb said. "The pencil's getting dull anyway. Do you have a sharpener?"

"Check the drawer under the plants." She dashed into the hallway, flung the cupboard door open, pulled out Ferris's swim bag and dumped a fresh towel in. Sheb ran with her, as if joining in a game. Then she made it to the front door and opened it, just as Phoebe was about to hit the doorbell a second time.

"Hey!" Hailey said and held out the bag, suddenly realizing her cheeks felt hot. "Here you go! Thanks again and have fun at the pool."

Phoebe took the bag, but didn't step back. Instead, she ran her hand over Sheb's soft ears, and her eyebrows rose as she searched Hailey's face.

"Caleb's here?" Phoebe asked. She looked past Hailey into the house. "Does that mean everything went really well at coffee this morning? Did you get your phone back?"

"What?" Hailey floundered for an answer. Had Phoebe and Daryl not heard about the Goats shooting a clerk and the mall being shut down? "Actually, there was another robbery while we were there."

Phoebe's expression turned to one of shock, and Hailey filled her in as gently as she could, skipping over any parts of the story that might upset her friend, like Delia being shot. But still, Phoebe's face paled and Hailey felt bad for taking the happy twinkle away from the bride-to-be's eyes.

"We had no idea," Phoebe said. "We both agreed to leave our phones behind today. Daryl showed up with flowers a couple of hours ago and told me he'd booked the day off work to help me with final wedding and honeymoon errands."

"Like buying yourself new clothes for the boat?" Hailey asked, lightly

"I wasn't supposed to tell anyone about that." Phoebe frowned. Then, just as quickly her smile brightened. "Apparently, he ordered some really wonderful engraved gifts for the wedding party, and I'm excited to see them."

And Daryl had taken a day off, without his phone, for this? That was hard to believe. The man had seemed addicted to his online trading and afraid to miss an opportunity to make money. Then again, he also seemed to genuinely adore Phoebe.

Phoebe glanced back at Daryl in the SUV. He leaned out the vehicle window.

"Everything okay?" Daryl called. "What happened?"

"It's okay," Hailey called back. "Phoebe will fill you in, I'm sure. You guys just focus on enjoying your day. I'll see you after swimming."

As Phoebe gave a hug, her voice dropped. "I'm kind of hoping to give Caleb a tiny role in the wedding," she said, softly. "Just to sit in the front row and hold a picture of Matty, so it's like my brother is there. My godmother is going to be holding my mom's picture."

"Sounds wonderful," Hailey said,

"Really?" Phoebe said. "You sure? Daryl was trying to talk me out of letting Caleb come. He still thinks having Caleb at the wedding is going to cause some kind of problem, probably after what happened between you two at Renee and Lenny's wedding. But I've told I'm sure it will be fine. You and Caleb are past that."

"Totally," Hailey reassured her. She and Caleb were different people now. "Now, go have fun and thanks again for taking Ferris."

She watched as Phoebe and Daryl left. Then she closed the door and walked back through the living room as Sheb wandered off to explore the house.

Caleb was waiting for her in the kitchen doorway. There was an odd, inscrutable look on his face, like he'd just noticed a bomb and was thinking through how he was going to defuse it.

"I think Daryl is lying to Phoebe," she called. "Not about anything major. It's just that he claims he hasn't had his phone on him all day, and I've never met anyone more chronically online than him. It's like he's addicted to monitoring his online money trades."

But before she could even finish her thought, Caleb suddenly strode toward her. A Hollywood hero's smile beamed all the way from one chiseled cheekbone to the other. His arms opened wide.

"Forget them," he said, "let me give you a hug."

Suddenly, she found herself entangled in his arms. Caleb pulled her up against his chest until she could feel his racing heartbeat and felt her own match pace. He pulled her closer still, until she found her cheek brushing against his. Then she felt him nuzzling his face into her hair.

What was happening? What had gotten into Caleb all of a sudden?

Was he about to kiss her? And if so, was she actually about to kiss him back?

His lips brushed her ear.

"Act natural and don't move." Despite the almost playful closeness, his voice was an urgent and serious warning. "Somebody is spying on us, watching our every move and listening to every word we say."

"What? How?" Hailey gasped. Caleb felt her stiffen in his arms.

Her eyes darted to the window as if expecting to see a figure looming in the yard.

"Wait! Don't look!" Caleb whispered, quickly. "There are hidden cameras. I found the first one while looking for a pencil sharpener and who knows how many more there are. We've got to stay chill or we'll tip them off that I've found them. And if we do that, we can't trace the signal."

She hesitated a second. Then, to his relief she relaxed into his embrace and nestled her head deep into the crook of his neck. This was great, because it meant she was listening and not about to do anything foolish, which increased the likelihood of them catching whoever had planted hidden cameras in her home. But unfortunately, it caused the added complication that he now had the sweet scent of her filling his senses, reminding him of honeysuckle, rainstorms and home.

Then her hands rose up around his neck and he felt his heartbeat quicken even more.

Come on, man. Hold it together. You're not actually

holding her for real. You're just pretending to in order to keep a criminal from realizing you're both on to them.

"Okay." Her breath brushed his jaw but it sounded like her teeth were clenched. "I'm listening. Even though I can't decide if I'm more terrified or livid."

Fair enough.

"Also, I'm not exactly sure what standing here hugging in my living room is going to do," she added.

There was something both feisty and defiant in her voice that almost made him chuckle.

Okay, so now that they were on the same page, it was time to figure out a solution. Ironically, if his friends in the task force weren't out of cell phone range, he probably never would've asked Hailey to talk through the case with him. Let alone been in her home long enough to realize someone had infiltrated and bugged it.

I don't know what's going on here, God. But it's clear that somebody is definitely targeting Hailey personally.

This wasn't a case of her taking a drugged drink that had been intended for somebody else. This was personal. The danger was in her home.

Hailey was still waiting for him to come up with an explanation, strategy and plan. He slipped his hands down to her waist, hoping to find a more relaxed way of holding her that would allow them to keep whispering without whoever had planted the cameras overhearing or realizing they'd been discovered—and without distracting his own mind or doing anything wonky to his now-racing pulse.

The new position didn't help his heart rate any.

"I'm afraid I looked right at the first camera I found," Caleb said. "I peered straight into the lens, I'm embarrassed to say. So unfortunately, whoever is watching us probably suspects I found it."

"Aah," Hailey said as understanding seemed to dawn. "So, if you'd grabbed me and dashed outside, they'd know for certain that you'd found it and cut the signal somehow?"

"Yup, pretty much." Caleb shifted his shoulders and her cheek rested against his chest. "We don't want to risk them cutting the signal until we can trace it. It's also possible they're motion-sensored, so if we leave the house the signal will cut automatically. I then found a second above the hallway door frame. I can only guess there are more."

Hailey sucked in a harsh breath.

"Don't beat yourself up for not finding them," he added, quickly. "They're really tiny. About the size of a dime. Thankfully, the microphones aren't sensitive enough to pick up whispers."

"But somebody was definitely listening in on that whole brainstorming exercise we just did in the kitchen," she said.

"I'm afraid so." Now the criminals knew exactly what they were thinking and how close they were to catching them.

"And you're saying I can't just tear the house apart looking for them and stomp them into pieces," Hailey said, and sighed.

"It's your home," Caleb admitted. "I can't stop you. But if you do, there's a good likelihood that they'll switch the cameras off, wipe the serves and disappear without a trace." She nodded and the top of her head brushed against his chin. "But as long as they're up and running, a police tech expert can track the signal back to the source and nab then."

"So, we make small talk for the cameras while you figure out how to track them," she said. "Got it."

Suddenly, a long, beautiful peal of laughter came from Hailey's lips, as if he'd just whispered the world's most adorable joke in her ears. She smacked him playfully on the arm, pushed away from him and brushed the lightest kiss over his cheek. His skin was still tingling as she flopped down on her couch, between an array of mismatched pillows and blankets.

"Come sit," she said. "I want to tell you all about the wedding."

She patted the couch beside her. Then laughed again as Sheb leaped up, plopped his head on her lap and rolled over onto his back, obviously thinking the invitation was for him.

Hailey launched into a remarkably natural-sounding monologue about the wedding.

Now, all he had to do was put their distraction into action. He couldn't exactly call anyone, or the microphones would pick it up.

Instinctively, he rapidly typed out an emergency message to the team explaining where he was and what was happening, along with the fact he was worried that the feed might be cut when they left the house. Then he waited. The only real reason he could think that someone might want to target Hailey was the fact she'd seen the Goats twice and lived. Maybe they wanted to know what she'd seen. In which case, the long conversation they'd just had in the kitchen had practically done the criminals' job for them. He gritted his teeth and waited for his teammates to see his message. Nobody did. They must all still be in the forest and out of cell phone range.

"… The trick was finding a color scheme that works for everyone," Hailey went on. "Renee and I are the only bridesmaids. Lenny and Daryl's cousin are standing up for him. But we've got five kids, ranging in age between a few months old to six years old." She ticked them off on her hands. "River, Lake, Fisher, Luna and of course Ferris."

Help me Lord, I need my team. I can't do this alone.

Suddenly, his mind suddenly filled with the simple and modest wedding that Gemma and Patrick had had at Patrick and his son Tristan's home on Manitoulin Island three weeks ago.

"Remember to pour just as much dedication and joy into your life outside this job as you to your work for this task force," Finnick had told them all. "We were made by God for more than work, and it's important to find life and meaning outside your job."

Truth was, Caleb didn't. He skipped church to work late. He didn't have a social life, let alone a romantic one. After Matty had died and his relationship with Hailey had ended, it had seemed easier and safer to just live for the job.

Which had meant cutting out the one person who could help him most right now.

Quickly, he cut and pasted the message he'd sent to his team into a text to his father and hit Send. Hailey's home phone rang almost instantly. She glanced at the screen. "Hey, it's your mom!"

Instantly, relief poured over Caleb's shoulders and he nodded subtly to try to answer the question floating silently in her eyes. "Answer it. Let's see what she wants."

Hailey reached over and picked up the phone. Even without her having to put it on speaker, he could hear his mother's bubbly voice filtering in down the line, inviting Hailey and Ferris over for dinner and to also stay the night.

At the same time, Caleb's dad was texting him back rapid-fire, letting him know that he'd gotten the message and was in the process of mobilizing a tech team to trace where the camera signals were being monitored from. Caleb had never been the kind of guy to run to his parents for help—even when the sensible thing to do would be to call the local police. As a teenager, he'd preferred to fight his own battles, live without the money some unknown person had managed to take from his wallet or even hike a few miles in the rain when his car was stolen than call on Mom and Dad. As an only child, his mother had already doted on him more than he was comfortable with. Guys like Daryl and Lenny had already teased him and called him pampered because of who his dad was. The last thing he wanted was to give them a reason for accusing him of getting special treatment.

But if here was ever a time to call them for help, this was it. His dad was the chief of police. His mom was a social worker. There was nothing honorable about turning down help.

And now here, a two-front rescue mission was unfolding in front of his eyes. His mother and Hailey were quickly making plans to meet up at the pool, pick up Ferris and head back to the Perry home for dinner. Meanwhile, his father was marshaling a police tech team to identify and trace the signal and track down who had bugged Hailey's home, before coming in and sweeping it clean of cameras and listening devices.

Within a few minutes, Hailey had ended the call, gotten up and was the putting some things together in an overnight bag for her and Ferris. Moments later, his father confirmed that a tech had found an unidentified signal emanating from Hailey's house. Now, all Caleb had to do was keep the cameras and recording devices running long enough for police to track the signal.

"I've got to go pick up Ferris," Hailey said. "But I know you probably have some really important stuff to do, so feel free to stay here, make calls and do whatever you need to do."

"Will do." He smiled as widely as he could and gave her a long hug.

"We got this," he whispered in her ear. "Don't worry, we'll catch whoever did this and it'll all be over soon."

Then Hailey pulled away and started for the door before stopping and turning back.

"Oh, can we agree to keep this whole thing between us secret for a while?" she asked, loudly, waving her hand back and forth in the empty space between them. "It's Phoebe and Daryl's special weekend and I don't want to complicate that with people thinking we're back together as a couple. So, I'm not going to be snuggling up to you in public or telling anyone at all."

"Totally." Caleb's voice rose too. "As far as everybody knows, we're strictly friends. Nothing more."

Smart thinking. Now, whoever was behind the cameras wouldn't be suspicious when they saw Caleb and Hailey going back to treating each other the same casual way they had before, without any more of those lingering hugs that somehow made his pulse go galloping.

Then Hailey left, and he was alone in her home with Sheb, who was still lying on her couch and now snoring loudly. All righty, now to put on a realistic show for the cameras. He opened the voice memo app on his phone and began to monologue notes about a previous stolen valor case his team had investigated and the various pawnshops a serial killer con man might've fenced things, hoping the Goats would be interested. But before more than a few minutes had passed, Sheb sat up and woofed, and Caleb looked out the window to see his father's Chief of Police SUV pull into the driveway, along with two unmarked police vehicles.

He signaled Sheb to join him, then opened the door and met his dad on the front step.

"Good news or bad?" Caleb asked, as he and his dad greeted each other.

"Mixed bag, but not bad," Sylvester said. "The signal's gone and whoever planted the devices started trying to erase all their online footprints. Fortunately, I've got my best people on the team."

They stepped to the side and waited as four computer techs entered the home and started to sweep it for cameras and other types of bugs.

"Thanks for this," Caleb said, "and for everything that you and Mom have done to take care of Hailey and Ferris."

"No problem," the chief said and reached down to greet Sheb as the dog butted him in the leg. "It's what I'm here for."

For a long moment, the two Perry men stood side by side and watched through the door as police techs moved slowly from room to room, searching for devices. In the end, they found five cameras total. Further analysis on the signal from the tech team said they seemed to have been planted in the hours following Hailey's car crash, when she was still in the hospital.

They narrowed the signal's source down to a three-mile radius in Thunder Bay. All in all, it took almost two hours to completely confirm Hailey's home was clear. Then finally, things were wrapped up, the police techs left, and Caleb got in his truck with Sheb and followed his father back to his family home. They stopped by his motel to grab some of his and Sheb's stuff on the way. Even though he knew Hailey and Ferris would be safe in his parents' home, something inside him still wanted to stay close.

It had been years since he'd stepped through what had once been his old front door. The paint in the front hallway had gone from a pale yellow to a brighter shade of orange.

Some of the throw pillows on the couch had been changed and the books on the coffee table were new. But overall, the house looked, smelled and even felt the way it had when he'd left it last. A leafy salad and a fruit platter lay on the kitchen table, along with a large jug of lemonade. But it wasn't until they walked all the way through the house into the large backyard that they found Hailey, Ferris and his mother happily playing lawn darts.

Sheb looked up at Caleb and woofed, as if asking permission to go join them. Caleb smiled and told the dog to go. The K-9 barked and galloped down the steps and across the lawn toward them. Hailey looked up, met Caleb's gaze and smiled. He felt something leap in his chest. His mother beamed as gently as a lighthouse guiding him home.

Ferris shouted, "Sheb! Uncle Sly! And Daddy Policeman!"

The four-year-old ran toward them, with his arms wide as if planning to embrace them all at once, only to fall back on the grass in fits of giggles with his arms around Sheb as the Belgian Malinois barreled into him.

All these years, Caleb had expected he'd face some kind of lecture from his parents when he finally returned home. Or at least, deep conversation about how wrong he'd been to disappear the way he had and the importance of stepping up.

But instead, all that happened was his dad laid a hand on his shoulder and said, "By the way, I had a quick call with your boss, Inspector Finnick, and gave him an update about the cases we're working on, the cameras in Hailey's home and the fact my team is tracing the signal. You always used to be a bit of a lone wolf. So, I was glad to hear from Inspector Finnick that you finally became part of a pack."

Yeah, guess he had. And even though he hadn't heard

from his teammates in hours, maybe his pack was a bit wider than he'd appreciated.

For as long as Caleb could remember, his parents had a policy of not talking about work when they got home at the end of the day. He hadn't really understood why as a child, imagining all the thrilling cases his parents must be working and the stories they weren't telling him. In fact, it had probably taken Caleb this long in his life to begin to appreciate how nice it must have been for his parents to have a few hours every day that weren't filled with talk of neglected children, poverty, crime and murder.

So after they briefed Hailey quickly about the devices that police had removed from her home and how far they'd come in tracing the signal, Sylvester went to cook burgers on the barbecue, Hailey went to help his mother set up their badminton net, and for the first time in years Caleb found himself enveloped in an entire evening of conversations that had nothing to do with criminal cases.

Come to think of it, Caleb was hard-pressed to remember when he'd last read a book, or gone to the movie theater, or for that matter gotten all the way through a television show, hike, or church service without feeling that he had to check in about a case on his phone.

But by the time supper was finished, the dishes were done, the sun was setting and Hailey had taken Ferris inside to put him to bed after several rounds of goodnight hugs, Caleb realized with a start that his mind felt lighter than it had in years. Carefully, he built a fire in the backyard firepit, then sat on a long log, which had been carved into a bench seat on the top. He poked it the fire with a stick, sending tiny cinders sparking up into the night.

God, You know how my team is always joking that I'm the resident cynic. And I like the brain you've given me and how I often look at cases differently from others. But I've let myself become bitter. Please, don't let my heart go cold. Please keep my heart open to what You have in store for me.

He hadn't actually realized that everyone else had gone inside, even Sheb, before he heard footsteps on the grass and looked back to see Hailey approaching.

"Ferris has asked your parents to read him a bedtime story," she said. "Sheb's in there too. They may be a while. Mind if I join you?"

"Be my guest." He slid over and made room for her.

She sat, their shoulders touching lightly, and for a long time they stayed in comfortable silence and watched as the orange flames licked up at the darkened sky.

"This is my first time here since you moved away," Hailey said, finally. "Your parents have invited us over, of course, but it didn't feel right without first talking to you."

"Really?" He turned toward her. The fire danced in the depths of her eyes. "I had no idea."

"Do you know for all the times I've told people about our breakup," she went on and laughed, "neither of us actually ever said that our relationship was over and that we were ending things? We just yelled at each other, said some immature mean things and stopped talking."

She was right, come to think of it. Maybe that was why he'd never moved on. It was like a broken bone he'd tried to ignore and so it had never properly healed.

"I was a kid back then," Caleb said. "Yes, I was in my twenties, but I was immature. I thought I loved you—maybe I did—but then Daryl, Lenny and Matty would tease me about settling down with the first girl I ever dated and turning into my father, and I became so determined to prove them wrong and forge my own path."

"To go become a big-city cop, like Matty would say," Hailey said and smiled. "And date all the fancy city girls."

"Are you kidding me?" Caleb grabbed her hands in his. "I've still never dated anyone other than you, Hailey. After all these years, you're still the only woman I've ever kissed."

"Really?" Her eyes widened. A flush rose to her cheeks in the firelight. The back of his own neck grew hot. He looked down at their hands.

"I'm not saying I've never tried to meet someone," he went on, "but it never went further than coffee, because nobody ever compared to you."

"Truth is, I've never so much as opened the door on a future with anyone else either." Hailey's voice dropped to a whisper. She tugged at their linked hands and he leaned in closed. "I guess because no matter how angry I was, I never fully closed the door on you."

He laid his forehead against hers and felt their noses brush. "I never closed the door on you either."

Then he kissed her. It was tentative kiss. As nervous as the first kiss he'd ever given her all those years ago. But then he felt her kiss him back. Her hands slipped from his and slid around his neck. He wrapped his hands around her waist.

A loud and tinny rock song suddenly spilt the peaceful night air. He pulled back and leaped to his feet, so did Hailey, and only then did he realize it was coming from his pocket. His ringtone. He fumbled for his phone, accidentally pushing the button to answer the call as he did.

"Hey, man!" Jackson's face filled the screen. "Got a minute? We need to chat."

NINE

Hailey glanced down at the phone as Caleb tilted it up toward her. The man on the screen had a short and slightly unkept beard, and he wore plaid pajama pants and a T-shirt. A large German shepherd was lying across his lap. By the look of things, he was sitting on the floor of a rustic lodge.

"You must be Hailey!" he said. "I recognize your picture. I'm Jackson and this is my K-9, Hudson."

"Nice to meet you," she said. Then she turned to Caleb. "I'll give you and your colleague some privacy to catch up."

"No, no!" Jackson waved both hands at the camera as if trying to direct a plane. "Please stay on the call. I don't know how long the Wi-Fi is going to last and we'd love to talk to you too!"

"Who all is *we*?" Caleb asked and chuckled. "How many people are joining us?"

Even as he said the words, two more boxes popped up on the screen as more people joined the call.

"Give me a second," Caleb said. "I'm going to put you on hold, so we can get inside and transfer the call to my laptop. The mosquitos will be out soon and we'll be more comfortable there."

Not to mention, they'd be able to see the team better on a larger screen.

By the time they'd thrown some sand on the fire, gone down the stairs and gotten set up in the basement family room, with the laptop sitting on the coffee table in front of them, there were a total of five people and three dogs filling the four boxes on the screen. Top right, in the box beside Jackson, a woman with a pixie cut and was curled up on a couch in T-shirt and bright blue pajama pants with yellow daisies. A three-legged Australian shepherd lay stretched out on the floor in front of her and a tall man with an impressive mustache sat off to the side. His navy T-shirt had the logo for a private airport in Southern Ontario. Caleb introduced them as Gemma, a private eye, her retired K-9, Simcoe, and her new husband, Patrick, who ran a construction company as well as being local fire chief and volunteer first responder.

Bottom left, in the box below Jackson held a younger man in blue jeans with a yellow Lab at his feet, who Caleb introduced as his teammate Lucas and his K-9 partner named Michigan.

Finally, bottom left, was a dark-haired woman with striking gray eyes in a Ontario Provincial Police uniform. Caleb introduced her as Blake, who occasionally helped the team out on cases as their official OPP liaison.

"Nice to see everyone," Caleb said and smiled. He looked relaxed in a way that Hailey hadn't seen since Matty had died. "How are things going with the case?"

"Good," Jackson said. "But exhausting. It's a long hike into the campsite to where the remains were found. We're hoping to have dental record confirmation by tomorrow."

Caleb nodded. "Are you all still in Algonquin?"

"We are," Gemma said. "Finnick invited Patrick to fly up with us to provide his expertise in wilderness rescue."

She glanced over at her new husband and smiled. "Tristan is spending the night with friends."

"He's thirteen," Patrick explained with a matching grin. "He can't handle being without his phone for even a few hours, or the new friends he's made since we moved to be closer to Gemma's work."

Gemma reached for her new husband's hand and their simple wedding bands gleamed.

"Are we waiting for Finnick and Oscar?" Lucas asked.

"Inspector Ethan Finnick is our boss," Caleb explained to Hailey. "Oscar is an undercover agent. None of us have ever seen his face. But Finnick sometimes includes him in cases."

"Oscar is deep undercover somewhere," Gemma added.

"Finnick is currently meeting with the police commissioner," Jackson added, "and I did send Oscar an invite but he didn't reply."

"Oscar is pretty mysterious," Caleb pretended to whisper. Hailey chuckled and leaned in closer to him on the couch. Their shoulders touched.

Two sets of footsteps sounded on the other side of the door coming down the basement stairs. The first was a quick patter of paws accompanied by a jangling of dog tags, followed by Sheb rounding the corner and making a beeline for the where Caleb had left his dog bed.

The second set of footsteps was slower, but Hailey could instinctively feel the weight of their approach, just as deeply as when they'd all heard them coming down the stairs as kids.

"Dad, hey!" Caleb jumped to his feet as the police chief walked into the room. "I'm just hanging out with some friends."

Sylvester laughed. "Gotta say this takes me back a few

years. At least this time I don't have to go searching behind the couch for kids who are out after curfew and start calling their parents."

Laughter rose from within the boxes on his screen.

"Please join us and meet my friends," Caleb said. He waved to the armchair beside the couch and then angled his laptop so that his father would see the screen. He tapped around the boxes as he introduced each teammate to his dad.

"Nice to meet you all," his father said and the others responded with a chorus of greetings in return. "I've actually spoken to Finnick a couple of times and formally invited the Cold Case Task Force to coordinate with investigating some ongoing cases, but he said your team was limited in taking any cases that weren't classified as cold cases."

Caleb's dad had done that? Something warmed in Hailey's core and she watched as Caleb's shoulders straightened.

"Honestly, I wish we could take whatever cases we wanted," Gemma said.

The police chief leaned forward, saying, "Your task force was formed specifically to do something very important that no other law enforcement unit in the country is doing. I've been following your progress closely and I've been unbelievably impressed at what such a small team has accomplished." He glanced at Caleb. "And proud that my son is part of it."

Hailey reached for his hand and squeezed it.

Jackson chuckled. "Sounds like something a dad would say."

"And a police chief," Gemma added.

"Just a word of advice," Sylvester said. "You're all still young—even your Inspector Finnick. My advice is when

God puts you somewhere, don't waste your energy being upset that God didn't put you somewhere else."

The police chief typed a quick message on his phone. A moment later it dinged. Sylvester put his phone away and crossed his arms. His eyes twinkled.

"I've just officially asked Inspector Ethan Finnick for permission to consult with the members of the Cold Case Task Force on a couple of open cases, and he's agreed." He glanced from his screen to his son. "The task force might not be able to actively investigate the cases we're dealing with here, but I would genuinely love to hear your thoughts."

Hailey watched Caleb swallow hard and felt her own breath catch in her chest.

Then Caleb pulled his phone from his pocket and opened it to the picture of the mysterious bearded man in the hoodie. "I'm sorry I never showed you this, Dad," he said. "But I spotted this man following me outside the hospital last night, and we haven't been able to figure out who he is."

"Hmm." Sylvester nodded and stroked his chin. "The photo's not good enough quality to get a hit on, but I did spot a similar-looking man at the mall today after the Goats' heist."

"Did you catch him on video?" Gemma asked.

"Not yet," Sylvester said. "But he can't hide forever."

Caleb pulled out the spiral ring notebook of brainstorming they'd compiled back in her kitchen. Hailey curled her feet up beside her and listened as Caleb began to fill his friends and colleagues in on everything that they'd written down, chipping in as needed to answer questions. Then together they filled the team in on the cameras and recording devices found in Hailey's home.

"I can fill in some additional blanks," his dad added,

"but not many. We can confirm the recording devices were installed after Hailey was drugged. We've created updated profiles of the so-called Goats that we've been circulating to local media."

He pulled open his phone and read, "Gruff, male, six-foot to six-foot-two, approximately 250 pounds. Billy, male, five-foot-eight to five-foot-ten, approximately 150 pounds."

"Could Billy be female?" Lucas asked. "After all, they're in disguises and are distorting their voices. You said this Gordo guy was being catfished by a woman named Hot Pepper online."

"Interesting point," Caleb said. "I never thought of that." He glanced at Hailey. "What do you think? I've exchanged some punches with Billy but you've probably spend more time with him?"

Hailey shrugged. "Maybe? It's possible they've disguised their height or build."

"Also," Sylvester said, "we interviewed Gordo at length. The photos that Hot Pepper sent were stock pictures off the internet. We have no idea if Gordo was being targeted by a man or a woman, only that he told the person Platinum Security's route schedules and staffing."

No wonder the Goats had been surprised to see her show up at the bank yesterday.

"What I want to know," Gemma said, "is how Caleb's cousin was murdered five years later and nobody knows who did it or why?"

Caleb snorted, as if surprised by her bluntness. The chief blew out a noisy breath.

"Okay," Sylvester said. "Matthias Pine was my nephew. I held him the day he was born, and his mother, Stephanie, was my sister. So, on a personal level, nobody was more invested in solving this case than me."

The chief turned and looked at Caleb and Hailey.

"Maybe I should've sat you both down and talked about this case sooner," Sylvester said to them, "knowing how important he was to both of you. But please know that while I haven't read you in on everything going on in our confidential investigation that doesn't mean there's some big conspiracy not to solve the case or a major clue we've overlooked."

Then the turned back to the group.

"We had a young man in his early twenties who went to a very large wedding with over three hundred guests. At some point, somebody spiked his drink with over-the-counter sleeping pills. We don't know when his drink was spiked, because he could've consumed it all at once or drunk it later in the night. But we do know that he was in his friend Leonard's wedding party, and his groomsman's gift was a silver flask."

Caleb and Hailey exchanged another glance. This was the first she was hearing of it, and she suspected it was the first Caleb was too.

"Did you ever see him with a flask?" Hailey asked. "I didn't."

"Me neither," Caleb admitted.

Then again, neither of them had been in the wedding party. So, to ask what groomsman's gift Lenny and Renee had given Matty literally never crossed her mind.

"We assume the flask is how he was spiked," Sylvester went on, "as none of the glasses we tested at the wedding venue or the diner showed up any drug residue. But we don't know for sure, as the flask was never found. Maybe it fell out of the car and ended up in the lake. The car was found upside down in Lake Superior with its windows down. There's also still no lead on who deposited the gift basket outside Phoebe's home."

"So, we don't know if they were targeting Phoebe," Caleb added, "or if they somehow knew that Hailey would be there and that she was the only one who'd drink enough of a sour grapefruit drink to feel the effects of the drugs. It's still possible they're both targets."

"So, either we're dealing with a very foolish criminal who launched a random attack," Jackson said, "or a very smart and targeted one."

"Is Hailey the only solid link we've got between Matty and the Goats?" Lucas asked.

"As far as we know," Sylvester said. "But the Goats did try poisoning in the first two cases. In the first they slipped an unknown substance in a security guard's soup. It was the only thing he consumed and he was incredibly sick after eating it. But it left his system before we could test for it, and unfortunately he'd flushed the soup. For the second, they tried to pipe carbon monoxide through the vents and knock everyone out. The most recent incidents were armed robberies. They seem to have been making things up as they go along."

"Are there any other patterns?" Lucas asked. "When we were dealing with a copycat killer last year, part of how we figured it out was finding the patterns."

"Not that I can see," Caleb said. "Matty and Phoebe's dad died in car crash when we were little. Phoebe doesn't have much to her name besides the Pine Suds cleaning company her mother founded—"

"And which Daryl helps run," Hailey added.

"Which Daryl helps run," Caleb agreed, "and which our other friends work for. Daryl is pretty wealthy though, and has made a lot of money in online investments."

"How much money are we talking?" Jackson asked.

"Enough to buy Phoebe a pretty nice ring and charter them a yacht for an international honeymoon," Hailey said, "although the honeymoon is supposed to be a secret."

"What kind of investments?" Gemma asked.

Hailey did her best to describe the arrows, boxes and symbols she'd seen popping up on Daryl's screen.

"Got it," Gemma said. "He's basically flipping junk stocks, buying online currencies and playing the market like a slot machine. It's barely a step above gambling, but it can be quite lucrative."

"What about Phoebe's first husband?" Jackson asked.

"Heart attack," Caleb said. "He had some serious health issues, including heart disease, and it wasn't a surprise. Matty and Phoebe's mother died of a heart attack too."

"No." Sylvester shook his head and leaned forward. "My sister Steff had a stroke, not a heart attack, and she had no history of heart disease."

Hailey leaned forward too, so did Caleb and it was like she could hear the collective creak of floorboards and couch springs as others did the same.

"Is that suspicious?" Gemma glanced at her husband, Patrick.

"Yeah," Patrick said. "I'm only trained in emergency response first aid, but I do know that carbon monoxide poisoning can mimic the symptoms of a stroke. Also, an overdose of sleeping pills can cause both heart failure and stomach upset. I'm not saying that the Goats' trial and error attempts to figure out the most effective way to rob a bank are definitely the same as how Matty and Steff died…but it is possible."

Everyone seemed to exhale at once as they processed what Gemma's new husband was saying.

"Was there an autopsy?" Patrick asked.

"No," Sylvester said. "Medical imaging of her brain

showed she'd had a stroke. She was in her forties and had both high blood pressure and diabetes, so they didn't look any further."

"Which is standard," Gemma said. "Strokes are a leading cause of death in women her age. Once medical imaging picks up signs of a stroke in the brain, it's very rare to look any deeper, especially if she has other risk factors. Less than five percent of all deaths actually get autopsies."

"After all, why suspect foul play when strokes are so common?" Jackson asked, rhetorically.

"Matty and Phoebe were away at camp when it happened," Sylvester added. "Alma and I went over and found Steff in her bed, after she'd apparently failed to show up to work for two days. If it was carbon monoxide or sleeping pills, whoever killed her cleaned up the scene and got rid of the evidence. There was no reason to suspect she'd been murdered."

He frowned and the wrinkles on his face deepened.

"Except that her son was killed suspiciously five years later," Sylvester added, "and somebody might've tried to kill her daughter the same way five years after that. Although I still can't guess why."

A long and stunned silence spread around the group as people processed the newfound revelation. Hailey felt her heartbeat quicken. She remembered how devastated Matty and Phoebe had been when Steff died. Was it possible she'd actually been murdered?

Sylvester was the one who broke the silence first.

"First thing tomorrow morning I'll talk to Phoebe and make an official request that my sister's body is exhumed and autopsied," Sylvester said. "It's very possible we are actually dealing with a cold case killer."

The weight of the single thought seemed to hang heavy

around the group. Was it really possible that Matty and Phoebe's mother had been drugged? That would make Matty's the second tragic murder that had hit that family, not the first. Maybe Phoebe really had been the one targeted with the grapefruit drink after all.

The chat moved on to talking about Sheb's upcoming K-9 testing on Monday and Caleb's worries that the incredible dog wouldn't pass. Then Alma popped around the corner to tell Hailey that she'd finished setting up the guest room for her and that Ferris was fast asleep in Caleb's room.

Caleb stood as Hailey did. The video call ended in a round of goodbyes. Sylvester and Alma disappeared up the stairs. Hailey turned to say goodnight to Caleb, and for a long, awkward moment Caleb and Hailey both stood there and stared at each other like two disjointed marionettes who couldn't figure out what to do with their limbs. It probably didn't help that although his parents quickly left the room they couldn't have gotten that far up the stairs yet.

Should she open her arms to hug him? Wait to see if he hugged her? She'd announced they were going to leave their fake romantic closeness they'd used as a cover back at her home. But then it had followed them back to his parents' house...where it had somehow morphed onto something else.

Something that could lead her heart to getting broken again if she let it go any further. It was like she kept tiptoeing up to the edge of a volcano because she was drawn by the warmth, despite the fact she knew it had the power to swallow her whole and burn her to a crisp. She'd once loved this man fiercely and with her whole heart. How could she let herself fall for him again, if he wasn't ready to love her back that way in return?

Finally, Caleb stretched out his hand. She did so too, but

as soon as their fingers touched they both pulled away, as if something invisible in the air had shocked them.

"Good night, Hailey." A wide smile tugged at the corner of his mouth.

"Good night Caleb." She smiled back. "Thank you for being there for me today."

She turned and walked up the stairs, leaving him and Sheb alone in the basement. Despite her fear that his parents might be nearby, the living room was empty and dark, except for the gentle glow of a single lamp sitting in the corner of the room. Silence fell from around her. And for the first time in hours, she let a deep breath fill her lungs and then let it out again.

Lord, I need Your guidance now. Please protect my son, my friends and everyone I love from all danger—including whatever foolish thoughts might cross my heart and mind.

As she turned to go up to the guest bedroom on second floor, a sudden motion drew her attention to the darkened street outside the Perrys' front window. Was it her imagination? Or was there a tall man in a dark hoodie staring at the house from across the street? A shiver brushed her spine. Her eyes darted first to the front door and confirmed it was both dead bolted and locked. The she ran for the last lingering light in the room and switched it off so she could better see outside.

There was nobody there, leaving her to wonder if it had just been her imagination.

The pullout couch was smaller than Caleb had remembered, but more comfortable than he'd feared it would be. The last thing Caleb had expected was to sleep so soundly and so deeply, but he fell asleep the moment his head hit the pillow. When he finally woke up on Friday morning and glanced at his watch, he realized the hour hand had already passed nine and was heading towards ten.

He walked up the stairs with Sheb trailing behind. For the first time in what felt like forever, his usual run-through of the crimes he wanted to solve and the leads he needed to chase was interrupted by genuinely happy memories of playing with Ferris and catching up with his parents the night before. And then there'd been Hailey—facing down danger beside him, talking to his team, letting him get to know Ferris, as he saw what a wonderful mother she was. Hailey was so extraordinary, not to mention beautiful inside and out. He was still amazed he'd ever gotten up the courage to talk to her, let alone kiss her. And now, she was the mother of his son?

It felt like he was being offered the opportunity for a life that was more incredible than his jaded heart had ever hoped for. Let alone expected.

But he also knew that if he chose a future with Hailey, he'd have to give it everything he had. He'd have to be all in. Fully hers. Holding nothing back. It was what she deserved.

Was he really ready for that?

Was he even capable of it?

He expected to find everyone gathered around the kitchen table with coffee, juice, toast and eggs, and the kind of laughter, conversation and joy that had flowed so easily around their picnic table the night before. But instead, as he and Sheb reached the main floor and started down the hall, his footsteps echoed through what seemed to be a silent and empty house. The bright sun from the day before had vanished behind a thick blanket of dark gray clouds.

Then the front door swung open as his mom reached through and grabbed an umbrella.

"Oh Caleb, hi!" Alma stopped, half in and half out the door. "Sorry, I've got to work."

"Where is everyone?" he asked.

"Ferris has kindergarten," she said. "Your dad and Hailey both had work. But there's cereal in the cupboard and coffee in the coffee maker. All you've got to do is push a button. Everything okay?"

"Yeah," Caleb said. He'd had really a wonderful time with his parents last night, but there was still one topic he'd been afraid to broach. Better now than never. "Are you the one who sent me the invitation to Phoebe's wedding? Because it's okay if you are…"

The words failed on his tongue as he watched his mother shake her head.

"No," she said. "I didn't. I can see why you'd think I might. Because obviously I think you should be there. But God has been working on my heart during the last few years and helping me see that I can't push someone down the right path." She smiled slightly and pressed her lips together, seemingly suddenly catching what she'd just said. "I mean, the path I think they should be on. Anyway, I've got to run."

"Thanks, Mom."

His mother's smile widened and she slipped back out the door, leaving him with the distinct impression that there were a whole lot of opinions she still wanted to give him on what he should do with his life but was working on keeping them to herself.

Thank You God for my parents.

But if his mother hadn't invited him to the wedding, who did? He kicked himself for being so certain that he knew it was her and not asking her sooner. Because now, he had another unsolved mystery on his hands.

Caleb and his parents were invited to Pheobe and Daryl's rehearsal dinner that night. Hailey and Ferris would be there too. But what was he going to do with his day until then? Caleb was technically still on vacation, and despite the excellent conversation he'd had with his friends last night, they hadn't exactly come up with any leads that he could chase.

He made himself coffee, fed Sheb and ate some granola cereal out of a mug standing up. Then he took Sheb out to his parents' backyard and began to run the dog through his paces for Sheb's upcoming K-9 test on Monday. The sky was dark and the scent of pending rain hung heavy in the air.

Sheb loved training. The dog was as smart as a whip, the fastest in his class when it came to bounding and crawling through the obstacle course, and unbelievably adept at finding the training toys, no matter where Caleb hid them. Where Sheb continually failed was in communication. The dog knew without fail when something was wrong but could never figure out how to direct Caleb to it. It had been one thing to know in his head that less than half of all K-9s pups ever made it through training to join police forces, and the rest went on to live happy lives as smarter-than-average family dogs. But knowing it in his head was one thing. It was yet another to watch Sheb dash around the yard—with his eyes alert, his tail high and his snout raised to sniff the air—and wonder what would happen to Sheb if he failed his test.

They'd been training for about an hour when his phone rang. He glanced at the screen. It was his father.

"Dad," Caleb answered. "Hi! Sorry, I slept through breakfast this morning."

"I'm calling from work," Sylvester said, "I can't talk

long. I just wanted to make sure everything was okay at the house."

"Yeah," Caleb said. "Why wouldn't it be?"

"Hailey thought she might've seen the man in the hoodie watching the house last night."

Caleb's spine stiffened as sharply as if it had suddenly turned to iron.

"Mom didn't tell me," he said. "Why didn't you wake me?"

"Hailey thinks it might've been her imagination," the chief of police said. "I searched the street and it was empty. There was no evidence that anyone had even been there. I did actually pop in to ask if you wanted to walk the neighborhood with me, but you and Sheb were fast asleep. Don't worry, I had the security system armed. We were covered."

Still, Caleb didn't like the idea of Hailey and Ferris being in danger, and him not being there to protect them.

"I'm calling to let you to know that we traced the signal from the cameras hidden in Hailey's home to an office building on the outskirts of Thunder Bay," Sylvester went on. "We got there and the building is completely abandoned. No business has been based there for months. Whoever bugged Hailey's home must've somehow broken in, set up a server there and cleared out when they realized they were caught."

Caleb blew out a deep breath. "Another dead end."

"I wish I had better news, but I figured you'd want to know." Sylvester paused for a long moment, and when he came back on the line his tone was softer. "Also, I filed an official request to have my sister's body exhumed and autopsied today. I'm the trustee of her estate, but as Steff's daughter, we will need Phoebe to sign off too."

"Have you asked her yet?" Caleb asked.

"Yes," his dad said. "I gave her a call before I filed the paperwork. Obviously, she was a bit upset but I think she'll be okay. The timing isn't great what with the wedding, but I'm going to bring a copy of the paperwork to the rehearsal dinner tonight, get it signed off and hopefully have some good news for her by the time they get back from their honeymoon."

Caleb silently prayed that would happen.

"What's the building address where Hailey was being surveilled from?" he asked.

"It was 42 Hargrave Street."

Caleb looked it up in his phone. It was in an old industrial area on the east side of Thunder Bay. From the aerial view it looked abandoned. "Is the scene closed off?"

"No. There wasn't any sign of a break-in and police officers have left. No working surveillance cameras. For all we know, our criminals just parked in the alley behind the building and operated out of a van. The building is owned by an overseas conglomerate that bought a lot of buildings and lots in the area over the years but have done absolutely nothing with them but prevent local businesses from revitalizing the area and thriving there. According to the company's lawyer, they're cooperating fully with police and have given us free rein to investigate the block without a warrant."

So, while the owners might be foreign real estate vultures, they didn't sound like suspects.

"Okay," Caleb said. "Well, I might go look around."

"Figured you might," his dad said. "If you find anything, keep me posted."

"Will do."

It was a twenty-five-minute drive from his parents' home to the abandoned building. Sheb wore his official

K-9 trainee vest and sat up tall in the front seat, alert for any sign of trouble or an impromptu training drill.

A faint drizzle had begun to fall, turning the pavement an even darker shade of gray. The building at the corner of Hargrave and Main looked even emptier up close than it had from the pictures on his phone. Red-and-yellow signs hung around the fence, announcing it was private property and that trespassers would be prosecuted. But the measly security camera didn't seem to be attached to anything and the gap in the fence was so wide, he and Sheb were able to squeeze in without Caleb even having to turn sideways. A quick glance up and down the street showed more buildings in much the same condition, many with boarded-over windows or long-abandoned construction.

With its stunning lakes, towering trees and jutting rocks, the area around Thunder Bay was, in Caleb's estimation, the most beautiful piece of land anywhere in the whole wide world. But it was also true that the northern city had its own share of struggles with drugs, homelessness, corruption and far too many young people dying tragically. The great irony was that for all the talk about Caleb leaving his small town and taking off to the big city of Toronto, truth was he'd always grown up just on the outskirts of a very different city, Thunder Bay, which was just as much in need of good honest policing is the one he moved fifteen hours away for.

The lot around the building was so large he wondered if the building itself would've pinged on the tech's GPS if the van was parked in the street. He also noted that no doors or windows seemed to have been broken, despite that the place wasn't in use. In fact, the lock itself seemed completely intact. Had the owners left the building unlocked? Or had the criminals somehow let themselves in? Either way, the door swung open easily to his touch. He stepped into a gray lobby with a built-in security desk, faded signs indicating long-gone businesses and a bank of stairs straight ahead of him.

They started for the steps. Sheb sniffed the air. The hackles rose on the back of the K-9's neck as the low familiar growl began to build in his throat.

They weren't alone. Someone was there.

But before Caleb could even ask what his training partner sensed, he heard the thud of footsteps charging down the stairs toward them.

"Hello? Police!" Caleb shouted.

But the words had barely left Caleb's lips when he looked up to see a tall and imposing Goat in a gray mask with curling horns appear around the corner.

Gruff raised his weapon and fired.

TEN

Caleb hit the floor and shouted for Sheb to take cover, even as the hail of Gruff's bullets filled the air around them. He flattened his body and crawled for the relative shelter of the security counter. It was solid concrete, built into the floor and shaped like a badly drawn comma. He crouched, yanked his phone from his pocket and was dialing 911 when he felt the reassurance of Sheb's snout butt against his arm.

Bullets shot holes in the floor to their left and right. Chunks of concrete exploded into rubble. Was Gruff alone or was Billy with him? Their meager shelter was a lot better than nothing, but it wouldn't last forever.

The phone rang for a long agonizing moment. He heard the click of the call being answered.

"Officer under fire!" he shouted into the phone. "Backup required at 42 Hargrave Street! Corner of Hargrave and Main!"

"…ature of your emergency?" The voice was faint. Static buzzed down the line. "…can you confir…"

"This is Corporal Caleb Perry of the Ontario Cold Case Task Force!" he shouted as loudly and clearly as he could. "Requesting backup to 42 Hargrave Street! Gunshots fired!"

The line crackled again. "…ocation…?"

He glanced at his phone. He was connected to 911 but the signal was so weak he barely had a bar. Seemed the signal on the outskirts of town wasn't strong enough to cut through the industrial building, and no people meant no Wi-Fi and hot spots to provide backup.

The bullets stopped. Then footsteps sounded, running up the stairs.

He risked a glance around the corner in time to see Gruff making a mad dash up the steps. That meant either he was out of bullets or Gruff was luring him into a trap.

He breathed a single word in prayer—"Help"—and decided which risk he was willing to take.

"Officer in pursuit!" he yelled into the phone. "Single hostile. Male. Six-one. Gray goat mask."

He muted the call and shoved the phone into his pocket. He'd learned from Lucas's fiancée, Darcy, that even if they couldn't hear his voice, 911 emergency services could still pinpoint his location using GPS and send help. He prayed that they'd hurry. In the meantime, he wasn't about to let Gruff get away.

He dashed up the stairs and rounded the corner as quickly and quietly as he could. Sheb stuck closely by his side. He reached a foyer and paused. Sheb's snout rose and sniffed upward. Caleb listened and heard a soft thud above. They continued up another floor and reached an empty hallway. Doors lay in every direction. Silence fell around him. Sheb's ears twitched toward a door to their left.

Slowly, Caleb crept to the edge of the doorframe, opened the door a crack and then glanced inside. At first, all he saw was a long and empty conference room and wondered if Sheb's ears were wrong. Then he caught a faint breeze of damp air brushing his skin and realized there was a window open on the far side.

"Good catch," he told Sheb.

Sheb woofed back in response.

Side by side, Caleb and Sheb crossed the floor, moving as a single unit. Rain had begun to fall now, whipping at them through the open window. A clang sounded. He glanced out to see Gruff sprinting down the metal fire escape as fast as his body would allow. The steps stopped a few feet above the ground.

"Stop!" Caleb shouted, then yanked his badge and held it up. "Police!"

Gruff stopped and looked up. His rubber mask was crooked. His eyes were hidden behind an unsettling red mesh.

"You can't stop us!" Gruff shouted, in his disturbing and distorted voice. "You're nothing but a joke, Caleb! And when we kill Hailey, just know she's better off dead than with you."

Caleb shouldn't have felt the man's words—let alone been startled that this masked killer knew his name. After all, criminals shouted hate at cops every day and he'd been called far worse than a joke. But there was something so personal, so disdainful and ugly in the Goat's words, Caleb felt for a second like he'd physically knocked the air form his lungs.

I don't know who you are, or why you think you know so much about me.

But I'm not about to let you get away.

Gruff turned and leaped off the fire escape into the dumpster below. Caleb and Sheb ran down the fire escape after him. The metal was wet and slippery under his feet. They reached the bottom and leaped, just as Gruff was scrambling across the pavement toward the gate.

Caleb's body tumbled into the wet bags of trash, dull and momentary pain shooting through his body as the stench of long forgotten pizza crusts and half-empty soda cans filled his senses. He shoved his body out of the garbage and over the metal edge. Sheb scrambled out after him. He turned to see Gruff disappearing down a narrow alley between two buildings that opened out to a narrow back road. Caleb gasped and ran after him.

"Stop right there and drop to your knees!" Suddenly, a strong, beautiful and commanding voice filled the air as Hailey stepped into the alleyway. She was dressed in a sharp blue uniform; her long hair was swept back into a bun and a security guard cap shielded her head from the rain. The gun she held in both hands was firm and steady.

Sheb barked as if in triumph. Gruff stopped dead in his tracks, less than five feet away from the woman now standing strong at the end of the alley. The Goat's hands rose. And Caleb could see the whole man's body shaking in anger.

Then Hailey's unflinching blue-eyed gaze met Caleb's. "I'll hold him. You arrest him?"

"Deal!" Caleb called out. He signaled Sheb and started down the long alley toward Gruff. "How'd you find me?"

"Your dad," Hailey called. "He called me about the case and mentioned you were here. Police are five minutes out."

Thunder roared. The sky burst open and rain poured around them. A wave of thanksgiving moved through Caleb's body, along with the thought that when this was all over he should encourage Hailey to reapply for the police force.

But before he could take another step, he heard the sound of a tires screech. He looked to see a van speeding toward Hailey, with a white-masked Billy behind the wheel.

"Look out!" Caleb shouted.

It was too late. The van was flying so close to her body

that Caleb thought for a moment the driver was actually going to plow straight into her. She screamed and dove for the pavement, barely getting her body out of the way as the vehicle roared inches from her skin. The hat tumbled from her head. The gun fell from her hands. Hailey rolled, but in an instant, Gruff had leaped on her, grabbing her under the arms and dragging her across the ground toward the van, even as she kicked and struggled against him.

"No!" Caleb shouted. "Let her go!"

He pressed her body forward, running through the rain with all his might, ready to fight off both men with his bare hands if that was what it took to keep her safe. Sheb howled in fury as the K-9 charged forward to battle beside him.

Billy leaped out and threw open the back door of the van to yank her inside, like the vehicle was some kind of beast ready to swallow her whole. Then a gun flashed in Billy's hands.

"Not one step further!" Billy shouted. Water streamed down the lines of his rubber mask. "Or I'll shoot her right here and now!"

As if to prove he wasn't bluffing, Billy raised his gun and fired at Caleb past where Gruff and Hailey battled on the ground. His bullets flew down the ally and ricocheted off the walls.

Caleb ducked behind a garbage can and pulled Sheb to his side. If Billy kept firing, a stray bullet could kill any of them, including Hailey.

Help us, Lord!

Then Caleb heard the unmistakable sound of a motorcycle roar and looked to see the imposing man in the black hoodie flying down the road toward him. The figure raised his gun and fired.

* * *

Hailey was down on the ground fighting against the masked man standing over her with every ounce of strength in her body. Gruff was nothing more than a masked blur of anger and hate as he tried to grab her over and over again and drag her somewhere she knew she would most certainly not want to go. Sheets of rain lashed her body. The pavement was rough beneath her. Her elbow ached and she'd purposefully rolled onto her gun to keep Gruff from grabbing it, and could now feel it digging into the small if her back out of her reach.

Sounds crashed over her like waves. Sheb was howling. Gruff and Billy were shouting, swearing and threatening them. A motorcycle was screeching to a stop. Gunshots were firing on one side. Footsteps were racing. Thunder was crashing. Her own heart was pounding.

And above it all she heard Caleb calling her name—giving her the strength to fight.

Gunshots seemed to be coming from both sides at once. Then, suddenly, Gruff was dropping his punishing grip and letting go of her body. She rolled over onto her hands and knees, gasped and wiped the rain from her eyes, as her mind struggled to process what her eyes were seeing. The two men in goat masks were leaping into a nondescript white van and peeling away. Caleb and Sheb were pelting down the alleyway.

But Hailey's attention was locked on the tall and imposing figure who'd opened fire on Gruff and Billy, chasing them away. It was the same man she'd seen disappearing into the shadows outside the house the night before, and who Caleb had seen lurking outside the hospital. He was about six-foot-five. He'd taken off his helmet when he'd leaped off his motorcycle and pulled up his hood, and now rain ran down this face.

"Hey, you guys okay?" The man's voice was deep. He turned toward them, with the gun still smoking in his hand.

She yanked her own gun from underneath her, rolled up on to one knee and aimed the barrel straight at the center of the man's body.

"Drop the gun!" she ordered. "Now!"

"Hey, it's okay!" He raised his hands and let the gun fall to the ground. "I'm on your side."

"Since when?" Caleb shouted. "Keep your hands where I can see them."

He and Sheb reached Hailey's side. They flanked her protectively, as slowly Hailey got her feet. The aim of her gun never wavered for a moment. The tall, bearded man reached for his pocket.

"Keep your hands up!" Hailey ordered.

"I'm just reaching for my phone," he said. Then stopped, stuck both palms up again and shook his head. "Phone, call Finnick and put it on speaker"

Finnick? As in Inspector Ethan Finnick, head of the Cold Case Task Force?

"Finnick?" Caleb asked. "How do you know Finnick?"

"He's my handler," the man replied.

The sound of a phone ringing filtered through the rain. Then there was a click.

"Hello?" The voice that answered was male, authoritative and strangely curious. "Everything okay?"

Sheb's ears twitched. Caleb rocked back on his feet and shook his head in disbelief.

"Boss, I've got a situation," the bearded man told Finnick. "Permission to fill them in?"

"Let me guess," Finnick said. "Caleb's holding you at gunpoint?"

"Nope, Hailey is."

The voice erupted in laughter. It was a deep, warm and reassuring sound that roared from the phone's tinny speaker, joined by the sound of a dog barking.

"Finnick! Seriously?" Caleb was already running toward the phone, as if Inspector Ethan Finnick and his dog, Nippy, had physically appeared in front of them. Slowly, Hailey lowered her gun.

The man handed him the phone. Caleb held it up and Hailey could see the small image of a gray-haired man on the screen. The grizzled snout of a black Labrador retriever crowded the corner of the frame.

"You really think I'd leave you without any backup?" Finnick asked. "Caleb, meet Oscar, the seventh and for now unofficial member of the Cold Case Task Force."

"Oscar, as in the undercover enigma?" Hailey asked.

"Guilty as charged." Oscar chuckled.

"He's been working a case a few hours south of here," Finnick went on. "I asked him to pop by and keep an eye on you. Just as a favor to a friend. Nothing official. Not on the books. I'll explain more later. In the meantime, just know I trust him with my life, which means you can trust him with yours. I'll see you back at the office on Monday."

"You sent Oscar?" Caleb asked. But Finnick had already ended the call before Caleb could pepper him with any more questions.

Caleb turned to the tall man. "It's very nice to meet you."

"You too," Oscar said. He pocketed the phone, stretched out a hand and clasped Caleb's hand in a firm handshake. "It's great to finally meet you face-to-face. That was a nice trick with the phone outside the hospital the other night when you managed to snap that picture. I'm not used to being made."

Oscar chuckled and ran his hand over his beard. Then he turned to Hailey. "Sorry to scare you. Finnick asked me to keep a casual eye on you from a distance, make sure you were okay. I'm also sorry I didn't get to the mall soon enough yesterday to make a difference."

"No worries." Hailey took his hand and shook it. "Does this mean you're going to be sticking around?"

"I'll be around," he said. "But I've got to keep a very low profile. I can't risk blowing the case I'm working."

Faint sirens in the distance told her that help was on its way. Oscar glanced in the direction of the sound. "I've gotta go, and I was never here."

"Sure." Caleb still looked somewhere between awestruck and baffled. "Gemma will kill me if I don't ask if there's anything more you can tell us about yourself. You're basically a myth."

"Nah," Oscar said and chuckled. He strode back to his motorcycle. "Just deep undercover."

"And Finnick is your handler?" Caleb called. "I literally had no idea that Finnick had ever been anyone's handler."

"Finnick sent me undercover a few years back when I was working with him at the RCMP K-9 Unit." Oscar grabbed his helmet, shoved it on and looked at them through the open visor. "Long story short, he was my handler back then and when he switched roles, he arranged to stay on as my main contact with the outside world, rather than handing me off to somebody else. My cover involves a lot of long days of waiting for something to happen, so sometimes Finnick loops me in on cases to keep me sharp."

The rain slowed to a weak drizzle. The sirens roared

louder. Emergency lights flashed above the buildings, refracted through the rain.

"Again, it was nice to meet you," Oscar said. "Hailey, I'll be around after Caleb heads back to Toronto on Monday, and I'll make sure you get my number in case you need anything. Catch you later."

He snapped the visor down, started the engine and peeled off before they could talk any more. In an instant he was gone, leaving Hailey, Caleb and Sheb standing alone in the rain. Sheb shook his body from his nose to the tip of his tail as if trying to shake the falling water from his coat.

"Are you okay?" Caleb said. "Are you hurt?"

He reached out his hands to her. She felt them brush against her arms, inviting her to step in for a hug. Instinctively, she moved toward him, only to stop as the rank smell of soggy garbage filled her nostrils. She stepped back, shivered and suddenly realized just how wet and chilly she was.

"I'm achy," she admitted. "I'll probably be in pain tomorrow when the shock wears off." Hopefully, she wouldn't be visibly bruised for the wedding. She could hear the sound of law enforcement shouting and sirens still wailing from somewhere on the other side of buildings, but couldn't see them. "I'm guessing you called the police."

"Yeah," Caleb said. "Though the line was poor so I'm not sure how much they heard. I should call dispatch, let them know the danger is gone and give them an update on the Goats' vehicle. I should also call and give my dad an update since he knows we're both here. Hopefully, the line will be better outside."

He stepped away, pulled out the phone, called 911 and briefed them. She stepped back and looked around. Hailey couldn't ever remember having been to this part of Thunder Bay. But as her eyes lingered on the empty buildings, she felt something niggling in the back of her mind that she couldn't put a finger on. Caleb ended the call and turned back.

"Okay," he said. "They're sweeping the building now. I guess we go give our statements and then I've got to get changed. I'm really glad to know that Oscar will be someone here to look out for you when I leave," Caleb said. "Well, along with my folks."

"Right," she said, "because you're going back to Toronto on Monday."

And who knew when he'd return?

"Have you ever thought of reapplying for the police?" Caleb asked. "Yes, I know you resigned after Matty died, but it's been years since then—"

"And I'm a single mother," she cut him off, "raising a four-year-old alone."

He stopped walking just as suddenly as if an invisible barrier had popped up in front of him. He turned toward her.

"Obviously, I want to be part of Ferris's life," Caleb said. "He is an amazing kid and I really enjoyed getting to know him. I don't know how it's going to work. With my job in Toronto, I'll have to come back and forth, but I'll talk to Finnick, I'll pray about it and I'll figure out something."

Then they turned and continued walking toward the flashing lights ahead.

Caleb's words about the future continued to run through her mind like a hamster on a wheel as they reached the emergency services trucks, as she gave her statement to police yet again, and as she got checked out by paramedics. Then she left to go get her phone sorted at the mall while she was still in Thunder Bay.

There was absolutely nothing wrong with anything Caleb had said. It was good—amazing, even—that Caleb wanted to step up and be an active part of her son's life. It was what she'd been praying for. Yes, it would be tricky, complicated and in some ways far less than ideal. But she still thanked God for it and would do her best to make it happen, for Ferris.

Yet as she went through the motions of sorting her day, something about what Caleb had said left a bad taste in her mouth, as if she'd inhaled some noxious smoke and somehow singed her throat. By the time she drove down along the water's edge back to Amethyst Harbour, no matter how many mints she tried to pop or sips of water she had, every gasp of air she took still tasted bitter.

Caleb had held her hand and wrapped his arms around her. He'd rescued her from danger. He'd even kissed her. Was she really going to be able to put her complicated feelings for him aside to be the best possible co-parents to Ferris? What if every time Ferris ran to the front door, excited to see his long-distance daddy, Hailey's heart ached for the husband he'd never be?

Still, Hailey tried her best to push through her day. She got her new phone sorted, picked up Ferris, brought him back to the house where they got changed for the reception. She chose soft jeans, a light blue shirt and brushed her long blond hair down her back. Then—following a nudging in the back of her mind she couldn't put into words, let alone explain—she tucked her folding hunting knife deep in her pocket.

Ferris was a bundle of excitement as they got ready and headed over to the rehearsal. He kicked his feet, danced in his seat and sang a little tune called "Ring Bear, Police Dog and Daddy," which he seemed to make up as he went along.

The rehearsal dinner was set in a huge, beautiful barn at the very edge of a large hotel lodge and resort, which contained multiple rooms, halls, cabins and stand-alone venues. The rain had stopped falling, but still the grass was damp and the smell of wet leaves hung in the air. The barn was set down a long, twisting road that cut through the forest, away from the main lodge on the very edge of a tall jutting rock overlooking Lake Superior. Trees framed the venue, wrapped in trailing strings of hanging lights. Dark blue water spread out below them like a tapestry. A gaggle of children ran up to the car even before she'd managed to get her seat belt off, calling Ferris to come play with them, while her son shouted and waved.

For the next hour, joyful chaos ensued as the venue's wedding planner worked at coordinating when, where and how everyone in the child-filled wedding party was going to stand, sit and walk down the aisle. To her surprise, Phoebe and Daryl had invited close to fifty people to the rehearsal, including many of Pine Suds's biggest clients. And yet, no matter how many times Hailey casually scanned the crowd, there was one face that stubbornly stayed missing—Caleb.

Where was he? For that matter, where were Sylvester and Alma? They were all supposed to be there. Yet, by the time the rehearsal was over, catering vans had shown up to rearrange tables for dinner and venue staff were filling the barn with hundreds of flickering candles, Caleb and his parents still hadn't arrived. Also, for all the smiles on Phoebe's face and the times they exchanged small talk throughout the evening, Phoebe never actually met Hailey's eye and never let herself get pulled too hard away from Daryl's side, let alone into a private conversation.

"Can I have everyone's attention, please!" Daryl's smile

beamed as he stepped up to the microphone. He wrapped one arm around Phoebe. Her huge diamond ring dazzled in the gentle glow of the flickering flames. "As a special treat, we've arranged a special pizza and crafts party for the children in the main lodge, hosted by the resident kids camp program, while the adults enjoy a quiet candlelight dinner!"

Children cheered, adults clapped, and yet as Hailey took Ferris's hand and joined the procession of happy parents and kids walking down to the lodge to drop the kids off, she couldn't help but feel unsettling jitters run up and down her spine. The lodge was well lit, full of people and had onsite security. Ferris would be surrounded by his best friends and the party was being hosted by amazing staff who threw parties for kids for a living. She had no reason to be nervous about leaving Ferris there. In fact, he would be safer there than she would be back at the barn enjoying a beautifully catered rehearsal diner. And yet, she couldn't shake the feeling that something was wrong.

As she walked back with the others to the barn, she found her footsteps slowing until the people ahead of her vanished into the distance, and darkness surrounded her on all sides, punctuated only by the twinkling party lights hanging from the trees around her. The barn loomed ahead in the distance, surrounded by the gentle glow of the golden light streaming out the open doors.

She glanced around to make sure nobody was in earshot, pulled out her new phone and called Caleb. The stillness around her was shattered by the sound of a cell phone ringing from the trees to her right. She leaped. Instinctively, her hands rose to fight.

"Hailey! It's okay!" Caleb called. "It's just me."

Relief coursed through her body as she turned to see him stride out of the trees with Sheb by his side.

She ran toward him. Their fingers touched. "What are you doing here?"

"Keeping an eye on you and everything going on here," Caleb said. "Oscar's here too. He's at the main lodge, keeping an eye on the kids. He'll make sure Ferris and the others are safe."

"Thank you." She blew out a breath she hadn't realized she'd been holding. Together they turned and walked toward the barn. She even realized their hands were still touching. Not actually holding hands, just brushing lightly. They stopped in the shadows just outside the barn and looked inside. Caterers in crisp white shirts and aprons were laying out a spread of amazing-looking food. Phoebe was holding Daryl's hand and laughing at some story Lenny was telling them, while Renee leaned into her tall husband's side. "But why aren't you and your parents at the reception dinner?"

"They told us not to come," Caleb said.

"Who?" Hailey asked.

"Phoebe and Daryl."

"What?" She glanced from where Phoebe and her fiancé were dazzling their guests and back to where Caleb was standing beside her, his face half hidden in the shadows. "What happened?"

"Phoebe called us just as we were getting ready to go," Caleb said. "Daryl was with her and got on the phone too. Basically, she's decided not to help my dad exhume her mom's body and said that if he tried without her permission she'd sue him in court."

"Wow." Hailey rocked back on her heels.

"Yeah," Caleb said. He led her away from the barn to a wooded bench hidden at the edge of the tree line. They sat down and Sheb stretched out in the grass at their feet.

"She was really upset," Caleb went on. "She accused us of being unable to let go of the past. Then she started to cry and Daryl got on the phone and said it was best if my parents and I didn't come to the rehearsal or the wedding, because it was the Goats' main target, which could be why somebody dropped off the basket with drugged drinks at Phoebe's home. Maybe someone's after his money."

"Or he got in over his head financially and owes the Goats money," Hailey said. She watched from a distance through the open door of the barn as Daryl led Phoebe by the hand around their table and over to where some of their clients sat. "When we were in the SUV on Thursday, Daryl was telling Phoebe to text Renee to tell Lenny to—"

The words froze on her tongue as her mind finally caught up with why the Thunder Bay neighborhood they'd been in earlier had been so familiar. She grabbed Caleb's arm and squeezed it.

"Daryl told Renee to tell Lenny to expand the Pine Suds cleaning accounts for two whole blocks around Main Street in the industrial area of the city," she went on. "But you and I were there this morning. Those buildings are empty. There is nothing there."

"Except people trying to kill us," Caleb said. He blew out a hard breath and then pulled out his phone. "I'm going to call my dad and tell him what we found out. You go in there and see if you can get Daryl and Phoebe to come outside so we can talk to them. If he's in trouble, we can help him."

The words had barely left his lips when suddenly a crash sounded, voices shouted and terrified screaming split the darkness. Sheb growled. Caleb leaped to his feet. Hailey did too.

Together, they looked through the open barn door in

shock to see the Goats, pacing back and forth in front of their friends and family, as Billy and Gruff aimed their weapons at Phoebe, Daryl, their guests and the catering staff and ordered them all to kneel.

ELEVEN

"I don't understand," Hailey said. "How did they get past us? We've had eyes on the front door this whole time?"

Hailey's heart raced and her mind swam as she watched. True, the Goats were unlikely to have seen her, Caleb and Sheb hidden the shadows. But it wasn't like the Goats could've just snuck in past them either.

"Something about this whole thing is off," she added.

Caleb didn't answer. She turned and saw that he was on the phone, calling police and summoning help.

"Hello? Hello? Can you hear me?" He looped his hand around Sheb's leash, cupped his other hand over the phone, and stepped away from the barn, seemingly to get a better signal. "This is Corporal Caleb Perry of the Ontario Cold Case Task Force! We have an active hostage situation!" He rattled off the details and address to the police operator. Then he turned to Hailey. "I've got dispatch on the phone."

Her heart raced. "Are the kids okay?"

"Yes. The lodge is now on lockdown. Oscar has sent me a text confirming Ferris and the other children are safe."

Thank You, God.

"You got eyes?" Caleb asked Hailey. "We need specifics for mobilizing rescue."

"On it." She walked around the barn, slowly moving

from window to window, trying to stay out of the Goats' view while also getting the best possible look on what was happening on the inside. There were about forty-five hostages, most of whom were guests who were middle-aged or older, along with some younger catering staff and the wedding party. The Goats had them all kneeling in a line now.

As usual, there were only two gunmen. But their behavior was different this time. The banter was missing. They weren't even talking to each other. The flickering candlelight cast ugly and eerie shadows down the rubber faces, making the Goats look distorted, almost different somehow.

Billy was pointing his gun in people's terrified faces while Gruff went from hostage to hostage, taking their phones, cash, credit cards, wedding rings and other jewelry. Daryl had his arm around Phoebe's shoulders. Renee was crying noisily into her hands while Lenny knelt stoically beside her.

Lord, please may rescue get here in time.

She dashed across the damp grass from the barn to Caleb, filled him in on the details in rapid fire, and then back to where her friends were being held hostage. For a moment, she still couldn't figure out how the Goats had possibly gotten in. Then she moved around the back of the barn and saw there was a two-foot gap between the barn's wooden floor and the actual ground, propped up by thick supports, no doubt to keep the barn from flooding when it rained. They must've snuck in underneath and popped up through a trapdoor somehow.

But since when did the Goats target private parties?

"You're hurting me!" Suddenly, the sound of Phoebe's voice shouting rose above the babble of greed and fear. Hailey's heart lurched. She ran for the closest window and looked inside, just in time to see Gruff slap her friend hard across the face.

"Give me the ring!" Gruff shouted.

"It's stuck!"

Hailey watched in fear as Gruff tried to physically pry Phoebe's engagement ring off her finger. But it seems like her friend wasn't able to get it off. Tension was escalating quickly, like a fire that was beginning to flash and grow out of control. Daryl was pleading with Phoebe to just let the Goats have her engagement ring, even as she shouted back that she couldn't get it over her knuckle. Renee and Lenny were yelling too.

Even worse, Billy seemed to almost be panicking now. He was scared. Why? Of who? He'd been overconfident every time she'd seen him before. But this time, Billy was shaking like a leaf and quivering in the soles of his thin and muddy tennis shoes, which for some reason replaced his usual combat boots. Then, with horror mounting in her heart, Hailey watched as Billy grabbed Phoebe by her hair and dragged her away from the others.

"I'll get the ring," Billy shouted to Gruff. "I'll take her finger off if I have to. Just get the other stuff on the list and get out of here."

What list? All that mattered now was getting her friend out safe and alive.

Hailey glanced back at Caleb. "I've got to go help Phoebe! They're going to hurt her."

Maybe even kill her.

"Police are on their way!" Caleb called. "Four minutes tops!"

She silently thanked God for that. But Phoebe might not have enough time.

For a split second, her eyes lingered on Caleb's face as

she felt the words *I love you* forming on her lips. But she bit them back unsaid. "If anything happens, take care of Ferris!"

"Hailey!" Caleb shouted, desperately. "Don't do anything stupid!"

But it was too late. Hailey had already dropped to her stomach and was crawling under the barn. Her body slithered through the cold mud, coating her arms and legs with every step. Chaos still erupted above her, as if everyone was shouting at once. She glanced up through the floorboards, making out shapes and feet as best she could, until she could see the soles of Billy's tennis shoes directly above her.

"Hold still!" Billy shouted and his distorted voice seemed lower than usual.

"Don't—" Phoebe begged.

"I have no choice!" Billy shouted. He set down his gun and grabbed Phoebe's hand. A knife flashed in his hand. "I need that ring!"

Her friend screamed. Hailey yanked her hunting knife from her pocket, flipped it open and drove it straight up through the gaps in the floorboards, straight into the sole of Billy's foot.

Billy screamed in pain and fell. Even though the slats, Hailey could see the blood gushing from the criminal's shoe. Pandemonium erupted above her. Daryl was rushing for Phoebe and gathering her in his arms. Catering staff and guests used the distraction as an opportunity to flee. Then a bright orange flame flicked through a gap in the floorboards ahead and Hailey's heart stopped.

Somebody had knocked over the candles and now the linens were on fire.

Sirens rose in the distance now. Voices shouted and footsteps pounded as people evacuated the burning barn. Thick smoke poured through the floorboards toward her.

And above it all, she could somehow hear one voice calling her name.

Caleb.

"Hailey!" he shouted.

"I'm here!" she called back. "I'm on my way out!"

She gritted her teeth, turned around and started to crawl back toward the opening she'd come through.

It was only a foot ahead of her. Any moment, she'd be out in the evening air and running from the barn fire. Suddenly, the trapdoor opened ahead of her and Gruff fell through onto the ground, still clutching the pillowcase of stolen goods.

She and the dark gray mask were barely inches apart. Gruff startled. So did she—but she recovered first.

"Caleb!" she shouted. "Gruff is under here with me!"

Hailey's arm jutted out from her side and jabbed Gruff as hard as she could in the face. She felt his nose break under the impact. But before she could land a second blow, his beefy hands reached out and grabbed her hard around the throat. She tried to gasp a breath, only for pain to fill her throat as slowly he squeezed the air from her lungs. Tears filled her vision. Smoke from above stung her eyes. *Save me, God!* She struggled to fight back against him, but she could barely move her body as she lay trapped and helpless under the barn. Dark spots filled her eyes.

Then she heard a warm and deep voice calling her name.

"Hailey! Hailey, I'm coming!"

She heard Caleb crawling under the building toward her. Then felt Gruff's hands fall away from her throat. She could see Caleb and Gruff exchanging blows, grappling on their hands and knees under the barn even as the smoke grew thicker. She felt Sheb slide under her arm and knew the dog wanted her to grab a hold of his collar. She grabbed it with one hand and held on firm. With the other she reached for the fabric of the Goat's pillowcase of stolen goods.

"Caleb!" she shouted his name in the smoke.

"I'm right behind you!" he shouted. His hand brushed and squeezed it reassuringly. "Let's get out of here."

On it. Together, she and Sheb made their way out from under the barn, letting the dog lead her toward the fresh night air. A moment later, she'd slithered her body out from under the barn to discover that the cavalry had arrived while she was under the barn. Bright police lights filled the sky. Police had begun to cordon off the scene. Hostages were being cared for by police. She saw Phoebe walking safely through the crowd toward the main lodge with Daryl, Lenny and Renee, no doubt to hug their children, just like her own chest ached to hold Ferris. Emergency responders rushed forward to grab Hailey's arms and help her away from the burning barn. But both she and Sheb stopped a few feet from the yellow police tape and looked back, waiting for Caleb's face to appear.

Please, Lord, get him out safely. Ferris needs him in his life. And so do I.

Then she saw his muddy face and crooked grin appear from under the wooden beams. Her heart soared. A smile crossed her face.

"Hey! A little help over here!" Caleb called to the police. "I've literally got a crook by the collar and need some help bringing him in."

She stood back with Sheb as police helped him drag Gruff out from under the barn. His gray mask was askew and blood dripped from underneath from where Hailey had punched him. Uniformed officers pulled Gruff to his feet and handcuffed him behind his back. She scanned the scene for Billy but didn't see him anywhere.

Caleb reached forward and pulled Gruff's mask off.

And Hailey stared into the angry and ugly face of a total stranger.

Caleb rocked back on his heels. "Do you recognize him?"

"No." Hailey shook her head. "I've never seen this man before in my life."

So, the men who'd been terrorizing her this entire time were strangers?

"Caleb!" Chief Perry shouted. "Hailey!"

They turned to see Caleb's dad calling to them through the crowd. Sylvester hurried toward them, and they met him in the middle of the chaos.

The chief's big arms enveloped them both in the hug. Then he let go and ran a hand over Sheb's head.

"It's good to see you're okay," Sylvester said. "Both Goats have been arrested. All hostages are accounted for. No major injuries. Kids at the lodge didn't even notice they were under lockdown. It all went as smoothly as anyone could hope."

"Don't forget this," Hailey said, and pushed the pillow-case into his hands. "We recovered the stolen goods."

Sylvester smiled and looked down at the pillowcase.

"Well done," he said. "We'll get the evidence team to do a full inventory and then see about returning it to the victims."

Hailey cast one look back at the barn. Orange flames billowed from the windows and firefighters were beginning to converge on the scene. Then she followed the chief, Caleb and Sheb through the police tape and out of the crowd.

"Do you have any idea who he is?" Caleb asked his father, as Gruff was ushered to an ambulance in handcuffs.

"I've seen him around the jail and courts before," the chief said. "We actually cleared him earlier in the investigation. He's a local drug dealer and user with a very long record for assault and theft. Been in and out of jail for years. But he alibied out for some of the other thefts. Guess the alibis were lying or the investigation messed up."

Caleb frowned. So did Hailey. So much about this whole thing felt off.

Caleb leaned toward her. "Why do I get the feeling I'm missing something?"

"I don't know," she admitted. "But I feel the same way."

As they drew closer to the ambulances, she glimpsed a handcuffed man with unkempt hair who was getting his foot bandaged by a paramedic. The Billy mask lay beside him on the ground.

"That's Gordo!" Hailey gasped. Confusion swirled inside her. This didn't make any sense! "The Billy Goat I stabbed was Gordo? How? Why would Gordo shoot Jet in cold blood or threaten to kill me? Why would he bug my house?"

"I don't know what to tell you," Sylvester said, shrugging. "He claims a stranger online paid him to be Billy."

For this robbery? Or all of them?

Caleb frowned and turned to Hailey. "Why don't you go get Ferris and head back to my parents' place? Get Oscar to go with you. I'll see what I can find out here and meet you back there later?"

"Okay," she said.

He opened his arms and reached to hug her. But this time she didn't let herself step into them. The case had finally been solved, however unsatisfied she was at the answers.

Once Caleb left town, the only thing that would be holding them together was Ferris.

And it was about time she got used to not tumbling into his arms and imagining that one day she might belong there.

When she hesitated, Caleb pulled back and crossed his arms across his chest.

"I'll see you in a bit," she said.

"Sure thing." Caleb nodded.

She ran her hand over Sheb's head, then turned and walked down the path to the lodge to get Ferris. Any worry she might've had about being alone vanished almost immediately. There were enough law enforcement going back and forth down the path, she might as well have found herself in the middle of a uniformed relay race. As she approached, Oscar signaled to them from behind a pillar at the side of the building. He had Ferris on his shoulders.

"Mommy!" Ferris waved. In one hand, he held a roll of pictures held together with a rubber hand. "We made pictures! I drew a bear! This is my new friend, Oscar! He's a friend of Daddy Policeman!"

Oscar came toward her, then stopped, reached up and swung Ferris around and into her arms. As she hugged her son tightly, the boy scrunched his nose and began to laugh. "You're super dirty! Mommy, you need a bath!"

"The kid's not wrong." Oscar chuckled under his breath.

Oscar drove them back to the Perry home in a dark black four-door pickup truck, and Hailey was so tired that it wasn't until she was tucking Ferris into bed in Caleb's old room that she realized the last time she'd seen Oscar he was on a motorcycle. She wondered where he'd gotten the truck. It didn't matter now—and thankfully Oscar had offered to stay at the house until Caleb and his father arrived.

Alma had stayed home, away from the violence, and was overjoyed to see them walk through the door unharmed.

"Where is Daddy Policeman?" Ferris asked sleepily as she tucked him under the covers.

"Working," she told him. "But we'll see him and Sheb tomorrow."

She'd also have to check in on Phoebe. She couldn't imagine the wedding would still be going ahead as planned, considering the chaos. Not to mention they'd have to find a new venue, on top of the emotional distress.

Ferris pulled the blankets up even higher. She smiled to realize he'd somehow managed to sneak his roll of drawings into bed with him and decided to let him have them.

"I hope so," Ferris said. "I like him and Sheb the police dog."

"Me too," Hailey admitted. Sudden tears rushed to her eyes.

Lord, help me accept what is and be thankful, instead of letting my heart ache over what You haven't given me.

As she turned away, crossed the room and reached to turn off the light, Ferris shouted, "Mommy! Monster mask roar!"

She turned back.

And jolted so hard it felt like her heart stopped.

Her little four-year-old son was holding a Billy Goat drawing to his face like mask. The picture had clearly been drawn by a child. But the curling horns, red eyes and snout were unmistakable.

She rushed toward him and reached for it as Ferris lowered it from his face. "Where did you get this?"

"Lake drew it," Ferris said.

Lake? Phoebe's daughter was six. Where had she seen the Billy Goat mask?

"Do you know why Lake drew this picture?" she asked.

"No," Ferris said. "She called it clompy boot daddy monster because it makes clompy noises when it walks."

He moved his hands to imitate heavy footsteps.

A daddy monster? Had she seen Daryl in a Billy mask? A shiver ran down her spine.

Ferris glanced at her and frowned. "Is it too scary?"

"No," she reassured him. "It was a very good joke. I just want to go show this picture to Oscar, okay?"

"Okay." Ferris smiled and snuggled his head back into his pillow, apparently reassured.

She exited, closing the door gently, and started down the hall, where she found Oscar standing in the living room talking to Sylvester.

"Is Caleb here?" she asked.

"No." Chief Perry shook his head. "He's taking Sheb for a walk. Said he needed to clear his head."

Yeah, she understood that feeling. She held up the picture.

"I just got this from Ferris," she said. "He said Lake drew it and called it a 'clompy daddy monster.' Is it just me or does this look an awful lot like the Billy mask?"

Sylvester took the picture, looked at it and handed it to Oscar.

"I can see some similarity," Sylvester admitted. "It could also just be a red-eyed creature of some kind. You said it was a 'daddy monster'?"

"A 'clompy daddy monster'," Hailey said. "Every time I've seen Billy, he was in thick-soled combat boots. Then suddenly tonight he's in tennis shoes? What if it's because the man behind the mask is usually a shorter man? What if Lake saw Daryl dressed like Billy."

"It's possible," the chief said. He sounded skeptical. "But

we're also basing this theory on a four-year-old's description of a six-year-old's drawing. Maybe Daryl or Phoebe lets her kids watch the news. Maybe it's a character from a story that just looks like the Billy mask?"

"Well, there's one way to find out." Hailey pulled out her phone. It was after ten o'clock at night. The children would probably be asleep but Phoebe might know. She dialed Phoebe's number. It went through to the answering machine. "I know she's getting married tomorrow, but something doesn't feel right. I'm going to go over and talk to her."

Sylvester nodded. "That's probably wise. Go talk to her, talk to Caleb, and then we'll take it from there."

All three of them tried to give Caleb a quick call, but his phone went through to voicemail. There was a quick moment of negotiation, and it was decided that Oscar would drive Hailey over instead.

"As much as I'd like to go," Sylvester said, "I'm not my niece's favorite person right now. Besides, all we have is a lot of smoke and no fire. I'll stay here, keep an eye on Ferris with Alma. I'll also fill Caleb in when he and Sheb get back from their walk."

Moments later, she was riding over to her friend's house. Hailey's foot tapped the floor of the truck as Oscar drove. Her best friend was getting married tomorrow. Phoebe loved her fiancé and was already feeling defensive.

And now Hailey was going over to talk to her about a child's picture? What was she even going to tell Phoebe? That she should postpone the wedding until they looked into why Daryl was telling Lenny to arrange cleaning contracts for empty buildings? That they had some suspicion her wealthy fiancé was involved in stealing?

Lord, please guide me. Protect Phoebe and her family if Daryl is involved in something criminal somehow.

But as they pulled up to Phoebe's house she noted the lights were off. For a moment, she thought there was no one home, until a dark car parked across the street flashed its lights.

A woman waved enthusiastically from the front seat.

"It's Renee," Hailey explained to Oscar. "She and her husband are in the wedding party. Her husband Lenny is Daryl's best friend. They also work at Pine Suds."

Renee hopped out of the car and ran across the street. Hailey got out too and they met in the driveway.

"Hailey, hey!" Renee hugged her tightly. Then, as they pulled away her hands rested on Hailey's shoulders. "What are you doing here?"

Renee glanced past her suspiciously to Oscar. "And who is this man?"

"Just a friend," Hailey said quickly. "He gave me a ride. I was worried about Phoebe and wanted to talk to her before the wedding."

"Oh, it's too late!" Renee said and shook her head. "They decided to elope. Lenny and I are watching the kids until they get back from their honeymoon."

"Elope?" Hailey repeated. Did that mean they'd already left on the boat? She didn't exactly want to tell Renee her suspicions, and yet she also didn't want to let Phoebe jet off and get married without talking to her.

"What's wrong?" Renee's eyes narrowed. "You look worried."

Was it that obvious?

"Look, I know Daryl is Lenny's best friend," Hailey said. "But I just think there's something off about him."

"What do you mean by off?" Renee stepped closer.

"Like, I know he told Lenny to arrange contracts on empty buildings," she said. "And it's possible someone saw him with a goat mask."

Hailey said it casually, as if she wasn't even sure it was true. But Renee's fingers tightened on her shoulders. "Who?"

A child.

An innocent child whose mother is marrying Daryl tomorrow.

One who told my child and who knows how many other children.

A warning brushed Hailey's spine. A voice at the back of her mind said *Don't tell Renee.*

"Don't worry about it," Hailey said. She tried to step back and shrug Renee's hands off. "It's probably nothing."

Oscar opened the truck door.

"Is everything okay?" he began.

But a muffled gunshot split the night. Oscar slumped over the steering wheel.

Hailey gasped and turned to run. But before she could take a step, Lenny leaped out of the darkness with a gun still smoking in his hands.

"You should've killed her when you had the chance," Renee said. "Now we've got to take her with us and find out who she's told."

Caleb raced to Phoebe's home, with his father's backup emergency light on the roof and Sheb in the back seat. The numbers on the speedometer might as well be Roman numerals for how well Caleb was able to focus on them as he sped through the twisting rural roads of Amethyst Harbour.

Ever since the emergency alert had sounded on Caleb's phone, letting him know that Oscar had been shot, only one singular thought burned like a fire through Caleb's mind—why had he let himself ignore Hailey's calls and texts like that?

He should've taken her calls. He should've read her messages. He should've been the one by her side when she went to talk to Phoebe.

Instead, he'd been jogging through the dark streets with Sheb by his side, trying to deal with the confusing thoughts and feelings swirling in his heart. When Hailey had dove into danger to help Phoebe, it had felt like a piece of his own heart had gone with her, and he wouldn't be able to breathe until she returned. Later, when she'd crawled out from under the barn, the criminals finally stopped, he'd gone to hug her—only for her to step away. That sharp pain in that very same piece of his chest had told him how foolish that idea had been. He'd been serious about being in Ferris's life. But without Hailey by his side, it was like planning to live with just part of his heart beating. But what other option did he have?

Even as he reached Phoebe's house, the array of emergency lights and vehicles told him to prepare for the worst. He pulled to a stop and leaped out with Sheb by his side as uniformed officers rushed up to brief his father on the situation. Desperately, his eyes searched the crowd for Hailey. He didn't see her anywhere. Then Sheb gave a short and sharp woof, and he followed the dog's gaze to see an imposing bearded man sitting on a stretcher, arguing with two paramedics that, yes he had been shot but that no he didn't need to go to hospital.

"Oscar!" Caleb ran up to him. "Are you okay?"

"I'm fine," Oscar said. His face was pale, but his hand gestured wildly in frustration, as if the bandaged gunshot wound a mere two inches above his heart was no more than a mosquito bite. "I'm just sorry they took Hailey. I should've stopped them."

"Who?" Caleb asked.

"Lenny and Renee," Sylvester answered, jogging over to join them. He pulled Caleb aside to a quiet space, away from the others where they couldn't be overheard. Oscar got off his stretcher, wincing in pain, and followed. "The good news is we've already got them in custody. Officers caught them at the harbor trying to leave in a motorboat."

"The harbor?" Caleb echoed.

"Apparently," Sylvester went on, "they dropped off their children and also Phoebe's children at a local pastor's house, told them there was a family emergency, and they'd be back in the morning to get them. The pastor's wife didn't believe them and called Alma, who advised them to call the police. Lenny and Renee claim they haven't seen Hailey. They also say that Oscar attacked Renee and so Lenny shot him to defend his wife. They've now lawyered up."

"And we'll have a hard time making charges stick unless I agree to blow my cover and tank the undercover mission I've spent years on," Oscar said, and groaned.

"Even then, there's no guarantee they'll tell us what happened to Hailey," Sylvester added.

The pain in Caleb's chest grew so tight that for a moment, he could barely breathe. Hailey was gone and there were no leads? Lenny and Renee had taken her, but why?

He opened his mouth, hoping to find some brilliant lead or suggestion on the tip of his tongue, but instead he just felt lost.

"Renee said something about Phoebe and Daryl leaving for their honeymoon," Oscar said. "But she didn't know where."

"Daryl rented a yacht," Caleb said. "Phoebe told Hailey. But I don't know anything more than that."

"Well, that would explain why Renee and Lenny were at the harbor," Sylvester said, "and we'll alert the coast guard on both sides of the border. But it's not going to be easy to find her. Especially if they've crossed into international waters."

His dad sighed, and Caleb realized with a jolt that he hadn't seen his dad look this worried about a case since Matty died.

"I need a moment," Caleb told Sylvester and Oscar. "I think I'm going to go pray."

More specifically, he was going to surrender this whole mess over to God. Because Hailey had been kidnapped. They didn't know how to find her, and surrendering to God might be the only choice he had left.

Caleb wrapped his hand around Sheb's leash and walked away from the crowd and down the street, until he reached the lake. There, he pushed through the trees until he'd made it all the way to muddy water's edge, and dropped to his knees. Sheb lay down beside him and he slid one hand along the dog's back.

Lord, I've got nothing right now. I'm at an absolute loss. Hailey is gone. I don't know where she is. So, help me, God. It feels really hard right now to hold on to any kind of hope.

He stopped praying and silence fell around him. He stared out at the huge expanse of water spreading out to the horizon and looked at the tiny dots of light that flickered on the water like stars in the sky. There had to be thousands of boats on Lake Superior. Not to mention how quick and easy it would be to divert onto an adjoining lake or river. How would they ever find her?

He saw the helicopter before he heard it. A single white

dot of light was moving across the sky toward him and growing closer. Then he heard the roar of the rotors growing louder. Sheb raised his head and barked as suddenly the helicopter dipped lower, sending sand flying around them and tossing the trees. Caleb expected it to fly straight over them, but instead it stopped right above his head. For a moment, he was too surprised to even worry what this could be. Caleb stood up. Sheb leaped to his feet and woofed. A spotlight switched on above him, shining down on Caleb and surrounding him in its bright glare. A rope ladder rolled down. Its final rung landed in the dirt beside him. There was a K-9 harness attached to it.

Caleb squinted into the light and looked up at the strong figure leaning out of the open door.

"Hey, Caleb!" Jackson shouted over the roar of the rotors. "Want a ride?"

Caleb laughed in disbelief as his mind struggled to catch up. Jackson, his colleague and the man who'd become his best friend since Matty's death, was now hanging out of a helicopter calling to him? Caleb fastened Sheb into the harness, then clipped himself to the rope ladder, and held Sheb tightly as Jackson pulled him up into the hovering helicopter, keeping one reassuring hand on his baffled dog's head.

They reached the helicopter. Jackson pulled them inside. Gemma shut the door and helped Caleb into a jump seat. Lucas handed him a pair of headphones and a microphone so he could talk to the team, then put a pair of noise-canceling K-9 headphones on Sheb to help the dog block out the sound. The helicopter banked and flew out over the water again. Caleb looked for Jackson, Gemma and Lucas, barely even glancing at the back of the gray-haired pilot's head. Both Gemma and Lucas were on laptops. He didn't see Hudson, Simcoe or Michigan and guessed his team-mates had left their K-9 partners at home.

Caleb's mouth opened. Then he gave up on words and shut it again.

"I've never seen you this speechless!" Jackson shouted.

"What are you doing here?" Caleb called. "How did you get Finnick to authorize this?"

"Authorize what?" The pilot turned and glanced back over his shoulder. It was Finnick. Caleb's jaw dropped. Finnick's eyes twinkled. He turned back to the controls. "I told you, Patrick got me back into flying. When we wrapped up our investigation early, I thought I'd charter a helicopter, get some hours in and come up to see you. I picked up some friends along the way."

"We had no idea that Hailey had been kidnapped until we were half an hour out and got Oscar's alert," Gemma said, leaning forward. "Since then, we've been able to check in with local police feeds and get a sense of what's going on. It sounds like Hailey might be on a boat?"

"Daryl rented one for his honeymoon," Caleb said.

"On it," Gemma said and started typing.

"How's Oscar?" Finnick called.

"Very annoyed at having been shot!" Caleb called back.

"Yeah, that sounds like him," Finnick said.

Within moments, Gemma had found the website for the only local company that chartered that exact style of the boat.

"I'm guessing the owner didn't trust him," Gemma said, "because if I cross-reference the owner's internet signal with what I know about the boat and real-time satellite data, I can find it via a hidden, embedded GPS signal on board, which we can use to track it."

She gave Finnick the coordinates while Lucas alerted

the coast guard. Now, they just had to hope that Daryl didn't do anything foolish when he realized they were being tracked. If he didn't have a hostage on board, hopefully they wouldn't try to jettison her when they saw the coast guard coming.

"And we found it!" Finnick called.

They looked out the window to see a large pine-and-gold yacht sitting quietly in the middle of the cool deep waters of Lake Superior. A short man in a captain's cap was pacing the deck, shooting dirty looks at the helicopter circling above and seemed to be shouting angrily into a phone.

"Why isn't it moving?" Caleb asked.

"That would be me," Gemma said. "I figured anyone paranoid enough to put a hidden GPS in their dark web rental yacht was also the kind of criminal who'd install a fail-safe shutoff that enabled him to remotely switch off his yacht's engines."

"Like how you can remotely turn off a car that's been stolen?" Lucas asked.

"Exactly," Gemma said, "in case whoever you've rented it to chooses not to return it. Once I hacked Daryl's online data, it was pretty easy to see that he was close to a million dollars in debt, so I sent a quick anonymous message to the boat's owner suggesting he switch off the engine and let the man who might try to steal his boat get picked up by police instead." She glanced out the window. "Looks like he listened."

"Hang on, if Daryl has no money, then how is he living a lavish lifestyle?" Caleb asked.

"Illegally," Gemma said.

"Obviously," Caleb said. "I meant how is he pulling it off?"

"I haven't figured that out yet," Gemma said. "But Lucas

and I will do that and summon help, while you and Jackson figure out if Hailey's on that boat and if so, how to get her out alive."

Caleb looked out the window, then at Finnick. "How low can you get us?"

"Pretty low."

Then Caleb glanced at Jackson. "Ready to commandeer a yacht?"

TWELVE

Hailey awoke in a pitch-dark space that was so cramped she could barely move. There was a gag in her mouth, her hands were tied behind her back and she felt the sway of rolling water beneath her. Footsteps moved above her head. Jumbled memories filled her mind. Lenny had shot Oscar. Then he'd forced her into a car and held her down while Renee poured something sweet down her throat. Then there'd been nothing but dark waves of sleep, pulling her down until she was afraid she'd never wake again.

"Hailey!"

A voice was shouting her name at the edges of her consciousness.

"Hailey! Are you here?"

Caleb!

Caleb was shouting to her somewhere beyond the darkness.

"Caleb, I'm here!" She tried to shout through her gag. "I'm here! Find me! Please!"

But all she could manage was a faint whimper.

Help me, Lord! Please, help him find me.

"I'm telling you she's not here." Phoebe's earnest voice filtered through from somewhere above her. "I wouldn't lie to you, Caleb. I promise you I haven't seen her and I had no idea she'd been kidnapped. Are you sure it was Lenny and Renee? Maybe we should turn back."

"We're not turning back," Daryl said, "and Caleb is lying. It's bad enough that he and his dog somehow snuck on to this boat. No doubt to try to make one last-ditch attempt to get you to go along with his father's bizarre plan to dig up your mother. But now they're accusing us of being kidnappers!"

"I'm not accusing Phoebe," Caleb said. "Just you,"

"I told you, Caleb's not stable," Daryl said. "You need to cut him out of your life, Phebes. It's time to make a new start. You and me. Together."

"And the kids," Phoebe reminded him.

"Oh, of course the kids," Daryl said. "We'll go pick them up as soon as we've eloped."

Hailey thanked God they hadn't gotten married yet. The voices grew softer. The footsteps began to fade away. They were leaving. They were walking away.

"No! Don't leave me trapped in here!" she called out.

Then she heard the soft scratching sound of paws above her head.

"Sheb!" She shouted the dog's name as loudly as she could through her gag. "Sheb! Good dog! I'm here! Help me!"

"I'm calling the coast guard," Daryl yelled from somewhere off to her right.

"They're already on their way," Caleb said.

"Well, great!" Daryl said.

Sheb barked sharply.

"Good dog, Sheb!" Hailey said through her gag. "Tell Caleb I'm here."

"They won't find anything!" Daryl said. "No Hailey. And then they'll arrest you for stowing away on my boat!"

Sheb woofed again. Louder this time and more insistent.

"What is it, Sheb?" Caleb asked. His voice grew louder again.

Sheb pawed the deck and howled.

"What's under there?" Caleb asked.

"Nothing!" Daryl said. "It's just floor!"

"Not according to Sheb," Caleb said. "Phoebe, hand me that fire axe! Hailey, get back!"

"Phoebe!" Daryl snapped. "Listen to me! You're going to be my wife. Don't listen to him. Just go sit down in the other room and—"

His words were drowned out in the sound of something splitting the wood above her head. Splinters rained down around her. Shafts of light broke through the darkness. Then she heard Sheb barking in triumph as Caleb gently crouched down, reached into the hidden space beneath the floorboards and lifted Hailey out into his arms. He reached around her and freed her hands. This time when he embraced her, she held on tight, breathing him in, never wanting to let him go.

"It's okay now," Caleb whispered and pulled the gag from her mouth. "I've got you."

She looked around as her eyes adjusted to the light, as Caleb gently set her feet on the floor and untied her hands. She was in a garishly decorated stateroom of what she guessed was Phoebe and Daryl's honeymoon yacht. Sheb was standing proudly by the hole that Caleb had just smashed into the floor, wagging his tail. Daryl and Pheobe were standing by some incredibly tacky mermaid-shaped chair. Daryl looked angry and Phoebe looked shocked. Then Jackson stepped through a doorway somewhere behind her, pulled a badge, held his gun aloft and told Daryl he was under arrest.

"Who are you?" Daryl shouted. His face went red with rage. "Were you just hiding on my boat waiting for some signal to arrest me?"

Before any of them could react, Daryl yanked a gun from inside his pocket at aimed it directly at Hailey and Caleb. Caleb's arms tightened around her. Jackson ordered Daryl to put the gun down. But Daryl seemed to only have ears for one person in the room—his fiancée.

"This is entrapment! You can see that, can't you, Phoebe? I'm the victim here! I have to kill them. You see that, right? They're forcing me to do this—"

Daryl flicked the safety off and aimed the gun right at Hailey's face. But before he could pull the trigger, Phoebe snatched a golden seashell-shaped lamp off the table and smashed it over her fiancé's head. The gun fell from his hands as he crumpled to the floor. Jackson ran over, cuffed Daryl and read him his rights.

"Caleb?" Phoebe said, looking dazed but sounding calm. "I'm the one who invited you to my wedding. I wanted you there. But Daryl was insistent you couldn't come. He even tried to stop me from including Hailey, too. I guess because he was afraid you'd figure out whatever he was into. I'm sorry. I never should've lied about sending you the invitation. I was just afraid Daryl would lose his temper and I didn't want to be alone."

Then Phoebe burst into tears, and Hailey rushed over and gathered her friend in her arms.

In Caleb's experience, most criminals were a closed book, who held on to their secrets so tightly that even years after their death, true crime fans, lawyers and investigators wondered what crimes they'd really committed and why. Others were so convinced of their ability to talk themselves out of any situation that they gave the whole game away as long as someone was listening. Daryl was the second kind.

He started confessing to Phoebe even before the coast guard had showed up, likely in some misguided belief that if he pleaded his case hard enough, she'd somehow accept that all the stealing, lying and killing he'd done was some grand act of love. Then after the coast guard had arrived, Daryl had been arrested and Phoebe had turned her back on him once and for all, Daryl had continued to pour his story out to Caleb and Sylvester back in the police interrogation room at the Amethyst Harbour Police Station, into the early hours of the morning, seemingly unable to believe that he wasn't a good enough salesperson to win them over.

Daryl had started stealing money from Pine Suds when working there as a teenager. His motive appeared to be a mixture of being addicted to the thrill, resentment at others having things he didn't, a sense of entitlement and good old-fashioned greed. He'd taken advantage of Steff's naivete and kindness. Then once she'd caught him, he'd drugged Steff with carbon monoxide in order to be able to hack into her safe, and hadn't expected her to die. He'd continued to cook the books at Pine Suds after Matty and Phoebe had taken over the business.

At some point, he'd been forced to let Renee and Lenny in on his schemes because they'd been working there too and caught him, although Caleb suspected he'd quite enjoyed showing off his schemes to them, not to mention he was able to rake in a lot more money once he had accomplices. Only then Matty had gotten too close to figuring out that they were stealing from the family business, so Renee spiked the flask Lenny had given Matty at the wedding.

The fact Phoebe's husband had died, so Daryl could start romancing the boss, was just a stroke of good fortune. But then he'd gotten into debt due to some online gambling and dodgy trades. He'd never seemed to have enough money to keep up with his lavish spending, and between the pressure to keep up appearances and pay up some pretty nasty bookies, he and Lenny had started robbing banks and jewelry stores to keep financially afloat.

As for Pine Suds, Daryl and Lenny had basically turned it into a money-laundering business through inventing fake contracts for empty buildings they'd never cleaned.

Daryl had been Billy and Lenny was Gruff. Renee had been running intel and created the Hot Pepper account online to get money to Gordo, who she'd also blackmailed on to robbing the rehearsal dinner to throw heat off themselves.

Daryl had talked Phoebe into not inviting Caleb to the wedding, for fear the cop might dig into Matty's death while in town and find something.

Everything had been going well, until Hailey showed up at a bank heist where they'd been expecting Gordo, and Lenny was afraid Hailey would be able to identify them.

So, Renee had spiked the grapefruit soda in the gift basket, knowing Hailey would drink it. Hailey had not only survived, but she'd also continued to interfere with their work.

They'd bugged her house to try and find out what she knew. They'd bribed Gordo and another local criminal to pretend to be Billy and Gruff at Daryl's wedding reception, to both throw people off their scent and steal enough cash, credit cards and jewelry to flee the country—including Phoebe's engagement ring, which they planned to melt down and sell for cash to keep one step ahead of the people they owed money to.

How Daryl had ever managed to convince himself that Phoebe would stand by him, as he drained her family business dry, turned it into a money-laundering operation and fled the country, boggled Caleb's mind. Daryl's so-called love for Phoebe had been so selfish, as if her heart was nothing more than another treasure he'd managed to steal.

Despite Daryl's insistence that he, Lenny and Renee had always planned to return to pick up the children after they were settled in their new home, somehow Caleb doubted that the self-centered trio would've actually followed through on that, especially after he got Daryl to admit that Lake had indeed caught him sneaking around late one night in his Billy outfit.

The sun had begun to rise by the time the investigation had wrapped up for the night. After listening to all the police interviews, Caleb felt more tired than he ever had in his life. Not just because he hadn't slept or how grueling the last few hours had been, but from the sheer exhaustion of listening to someone lie to themself and others for that many hours in a row.

Lord, whatever comes next in my life, help me always be honest with myself. I chose to believe the lie that Ferris wasn't my son. I chose to believe that I wasn't in love with Hailey, because I was scared of giving up on my dreams and people thinking I'd become my father. Please, keep my heart open for Your truth.

Hailey left the precinct while Caleb was still in meetings, and according to his dad had stopped by to visit Delia in the hospital on the way home. Thankfully, Delia was doing well and would make a full recovery. Caleb drove home with his father, and as they reached the front door of his parents' home, the sound of joyful voices and smells of good food reached his senses. They stepped through the threshold to see his mother, Ferris, Jackson, Gemma, Lucas and Finnick gathered around the table, eating pancakes, drinking juice and coffee and chatting about the cold case they'd just successfully closed in Algonquin Provincial Park.

"Daddy Policeman!" Ferris leaped from his chair and ran to hug him. "Mommy just left for a walk. Mommy's missing the pancakes."

"I'll go find her and tell her about pancakes, shall I?" Caleb asked and tousled the boy's head.

Ferris nodded, then grabbed Sylvester's hand and dragged him toward the table.

Caleb looked down at his tired K-9 trainee. "Looks like you and I have a few more steps to take before we can rest."

He found Hailey sitting on a large rock by the water's edge, looking out at the golden sparkles dancing on the surface of the lake. She looked up, as if sensing his presence, and the most beautiful smile he'd ever seen in his life crossed her face. Suddenly, Caleb found himself running for her, pushing his exhausted limbs across the beach until he reached her. She slipped off the rock, he reached for her and pulled her into his arms and buried his face in her hair. And for a long time, he clung to her and she clung to him, like two people who'd been shipwrecked together and had just now found their new home on dry land.

Then he pulled away, just enough that he could look into her face, but not so much that his hands slid away from her body.

"I love you," he blurted out, before she could say anything. "I love you and I've decided to quit the Cold Case Task Force, unless Finnick can find me a remote role that I can do up here. Because I want to be Ferris's full-time daddy and I want to be your full-time husband, if you'll have me."

He let go of her and dropped to his knees in the sand

by Hailey's feet. Her hands slid to her face as tears filled her eyes.

"I'm in love with you," Caleb said. "Maybe I've always been and just needed to grow into enough of a man for you. I just know that I'm done lying to myself. The truth is, I still don't want to be a small-town cop. But that doesn't mean I can't find a different role for me, one where I can wake up with you in my arms every morning and fall asleep beside you every night. What do you say?"

"Yes!" Hailey said. Laughter and tears mingled in her voice. "I love you and I'll definitely marry you."

She dropped to her knees beside him, kissed his lips and hugged him tightly. He rested his head on her shoulder and for a long moment, simply relaxed into the feeling of their arms around each other.

Then they pulled away slowly and stood, and he filled her in on everything Daryl had confessed to, including Steff's murder, Matty's murder, trying to kill her and being Billy Goat while Lenny was Gruff.

"Phoebe's going to need our help healing," Hailey said after she'd taken a moment to digest all he'd said. "Also, we're going to have to be there for Renee and Lenny's children, Luna and Forest, while their parents are in jail. I suspect Phoebe will try to foster them."

"Yeah," Caleb said.

"Also," Hailey added, "I think you're right that I should try to get my badge back. I miss being a cop."

He chuckled. "You'll be an incredible cop."

His work-focused life was about to get a lot more complicated. But good too.

A sudden burst of barking drew his attention farther down the beach, to where Sheb was splashing in the water and seemed to be arguing with a seagull.

"What about Sheb?" Hailey asked.

"Oh, he's definitely failing his K-9 training test," Caleb said. "But I'm going to put in to adopt him as our family pet. I think he fits in just perfectly with us."

"I think so too," Hailey said. "We're a good family for second chances."

Caleb laughed again. Then he turned to face her.

"Thank you for keeping the door open for me," Caleb said.

"I always will," Hailey said.

She reached for him, and they kissed each other for a long and endless moment that felt like the first minute of forever. Then Caleb wrapped his arm around Hailey's shoulders, she put an arm around his waist, he called Sheb to his side, and they walked back to the house to tell their son and the others the good news.

* * * * *

If you enjoyed Caleb and Hailey's story,
be sure to read Gemma and Patrick's story,
Christmas Under Threat
and all the other books in Maggie K. Black's
Unsolved Criminal Files series

Available now from Love Inspired Suspense!

And discover more at Harlequin.com.

Dear Reader,

Ever have someone say something to you that then sticks for your entire life? Over a decade ago, I was talking to some people who'd uprooted their entire life to do development work in a remote part of Northern Africa.

"Most of the time you're just going forward, taking one step after another," one of them told me. "Other times, suddenly you find yourself on God's Moving Sidewalk."

I think of that analogy every time I'm on a moving sidewalk at an airport or amusement park. In my experience, life is like that too. Most of the time, all we can do is focus on taking the next right step. Some of them are really tiny steps too. And then in other rare times, we can tell that we're moving in the right direction, and sometimes a whole lot faster than we ever expected!

Whenever I'm writing a book, I always try to remember that all we're getting is a little snapshot of our character's lives. We're just popping in for a visit. But God has been working in their lives for months and years before we meet them and will continue to work in them afterward.

Thank you again for sharing this journey will me.

I couldn't do this without you,
Maggie

Get up to 4 Free Books!

We'll send you 2 free books from each series you try PLUS a free Mystery Gift.

FREE Value Over $25

Both the **Love Inspired®** and **Love Inspired® Suspense** series feature compelling novels filled with inspirational romance, faith, forgiveness and hope.

YES! Please send me 2 FREE novels from the Love Inspired or Love Inspired Suspense series and my FREE gift (gift is worth about $10 retail). After receiving them, if I don't wish to receive any more books, I can return the shipping statement marked "cancel." If I don't cancel, I will receive 6 brand-new Love Inspired Larger-Print books or Love Inspired Suspense Larger-Print books every month and be billed just $7.19 each in the U.S. or $7.99 each in Canada. That is a savings of 20% off the cover price. It's quite a bargain! Shipping and handling is just 50¢ per book in the U.S. and $1.25 per book in Canada.* I understand that accepting the 2 free books and gift places me under no obligation to buy anything. I can always return a shipment and cancel at any time by calling the number below. The free books and gift are mine to keep no matter what I decide.

Choose one: ☐ **Love Inspired Larger-Print** (122/322 BPA G36Y)   ☐ **Love Inspired Suspense Larger-Print** (107/307 BPA G36Y)   ☐ **Or Try Both!** (122/322 & 107/307 BPA G36Z)

Name (please print)

Address   Apt. #

City   State/Province   Zip/Postal Code

Email: Please check this box ☐ if you would like to receive newsletters and promotional emails from Harlequin Enterprises ULC and its affiliates. You can unsubscribe anytime.

Mail to the **Harlequin Reader Service:**
IN U.S.A.: P.O. Box 1341, Buffalo, NY 14240-8531
IN CANADA: P.O. Box 603, Fort Erie, Ontario L2A 5X3

Want to explore our other series or interested in ebooks? **Visit www.ReaderService.com or call 1-800-873-8635.**